TRIPLE M F

Slick Rock 10

Becca Van

MENAGE EVERLASTING

Siren Publishing, Inc.
www.SirenPublishing.com

A SIREN PUBLISHING BOOK
IMPRINT: Ménage Everlasting

TRIPLE M RANCH
Copyright © 2014 by Becca Van

ISBN: 978-1-62740-903-2

First Printing: March 2014

Cover design by Les Byerley
All art and logo copyright © 2014 by Siren Publishing, Inc.

Printed in the U.S.A.

PUBLISHER
Siren Publishing, Inc.
www.SirenPublishing.com

TRIPLE M RANCH

Slick Rock 10

BECCA VAN
Copyright © 2014

Chapter One

Cashmere Woodall glanced from beneath her eyelashes and watched the denim stretch over Bruce Morten's ass when he picked up another bale of hay and then lifted it with ease.

A shiver worked its way up her spine and she looked away from the man's delectably beefy ass. Bruce, or Brutus, as his family and friends affectionately called him, had been working in the barn for the last hour and for some reason she had a hard time keeping her eyes off of his hugely muscular body. The man was so tall he had to duck every time he walked through a doorway and his shoulders were so wide it was touch and go whether they'd fit through the space between the wooden doorframes. His eyes were as brown as his hair and he had so much muscle he should have looked awkward, but he moved with an easy lope which seemed to belie his strength.

He and his brothers Cain and Danny were running the Double M Ranch while the owners, Clay and Johnny Morten and their wife, Tara, as well as their two kids, took a much-needed long vacation.

Cash had started working on the ranch a little over a year ago to look after the horses. She loved her job because she loved horses more than people. She'd learned a long time ago that she couldn't depend on anyone but herself. People could be cruel and selfish but animals never had a bad word to say and showed their affection in so many ways. Love from an animal was unconditional with no underlying scheme or agenda. Cash ran the brush over the bay's silky coat. It always soothed her when she was brushing down one of the horses.

A noise near the entrance to the barn drew her attention and she bit her lip when she saw Harry Staff walking in. Harry was a very nice man and Cash had a bit of a crush on the other ranch hand but he never once looked at her as a man interested in a woman. He wasn't tall for a man, standing at around five foot seven, and he wasn't bulging with muscle, but he was handsome enough and she wasn't intimidated by him in the least. She watched his loose-limbed gait until he disappeared into the tack room near the back of the barn. Movement near the stack of hay drew her gaze and she blushed when she found Bruce looking at her with a frown. Heat crept up her cheeks and she quickly lowered her eyes and went back to grooming her charge.

Cashmere was on the small side for a female at five foot two, so any male who was heading toward the six foot mark or beyond tended to worry her. From her experience big men used their strength to hurt women and she tried to keep away from them. Although Clay and Johnny Morten were big men she wasn't worried about them hurting her. Those two men were so in love with their wife, Tara, and treated her like she was a queen.

Harry came back out of the tack room with a bridle in hand and when his gaze met hers he gave her a smile. That smile seemed to light up his whole face and made him look younger than his thirty-something years. Cash bit her lip and watched him until he'd disappeared.

"You know, he's never going to look at you the way you want him to."

Cash glanced over her shoulder to see Bruce watching her from his seat on a bale of hay.

"Wh–What?" Cash stuttered and frowned because goose bumps erupted over her skin and she had to concentrate really hard so it wouldn't show. *Why is my body reacting to him?* Bruce's voice had such a deep cadence it washed over her like warm molasses. Yes the man was handsome and sex on legs but she wasn't attracted to him at all. She was drawn to Harry. Wasn't she?

"Haven't you seen the way he and that other guy...David look at each other?" Bruce scratched his jaw with a huge hand and then pinned her with his eyes.

"What are you trying to say?" Cashmere snapped.

"Harry's gay, sweet cheeks." Bruce rose to his feet and slowly walked toward her. Because he was so tall, it only took him three steps to reach the outside of the stall she was currently working in.

"You don't know that." She backed up and moved so that Star, the bay mare she was grooming, was between her and Brutus.

"It's true," another deep gravelly voice chimed in.

Cashmere had been so intent on keeping her eye on and space between her and Bruce she hadn't noticed anyone else enter the barn. She turned to glare at the interloper and her heartbeat picked up. Cain Morten was leaning nonchalantly against the open gate to the stall and was staring at her. Cain wasn't as big as Bruce but he was still hellaciously huge. Where Bruce had to be six foot seven or eight, Cain was only around six five. Cash gave a mental snort. *Only* was an understatement, especially when the top of her head didn't even reach their shoulders.

"What's going on?" Danny Morten, Cain's twin brother, said as he too walked toward the stall.

"We were just trying to tell Cashmere that Harry preferred men," Cain explained.

Danny and Cain were identical twins. They stood at the same height, had the same colored light brown hair and hazel eyes, and their physiques were mirror images, strong and muscular, but Cash had no trouble telling them apart. She could see a slight difference between the two men. Cain had a slight tilt to his lips that Danny didn't and Danny had a small scar above his left eyebrow. Their personalities were different, too. Cain was arrogant and authoritative, where Danny was impatient and always in a rush. Bruce was the one that made her more nervous out of all three of them. He didn't talk much but when he did she couldn't help but take notice. His voice was one of the deepest timbres she'd ever heard and although he was always polite and tried to speak gently, at least around her, he was impossible to ignore.

"You shouldn't go around saying such things, Cain. If you're wrong you could hurt someone."

Cain and Danny gave each other a look and then glanced at Bruce. Cash had no idea what was going on but she didn't like the gleam in the three men's eyes.

Harry came sauntering back into the barn, gave them a curious look but didn't say anything. He took the bridle back to the tack room and came out again. Cashmere hoped he hadn't heard what the Morten brothers were saying because if they were wrong he could be highly offended. Cash had no problem with how other people lived their lives or what their sexual orientation or kink was. As long as everyone was consensual then why shouldn't they live their lives the way they wished? But she thought they were wrong about Harry.

Harry stopped on the outside of the stall she was in and the corner of the next one. He looked a little worried but he gave her a tentative smile. "They're right Cash. I thought you knew David and I were in a relationship? But who said I only liked men?" He glared at the other three men. "I like women, too. Does that bother you?"

"No." Cash sighed and bit her lip, all the while wondering why she didn't feel hurt. She was disappointed to learn that there would never be anything other than friendship between her and Harry, but she valued their relationship.

Harry turned to look at the three Morten brothers. "Can you give us a minute?"

Bruce looked concerned but he gave a nod and began to leave. Cain and Danny scowled at Harry as if in silent warning and then they, too, left.

Harry entered the stall, picked up another brush and began to groom Star's coat. Cash stroked the brush in rhythmic motions and waited for Harry to talk. Finally the silence got to be too much and she looked up to find him watching her. He moved around Star and took the brush from her hand and then put both brushes into the bucket near the stall wall.

"I'm sorry if I've hurt you, Cash. David and I knew you had a little crush on me but we also thought you knew about us. By the way I'm not into women at all but I thought that comment about liking women would keep them on their toes." Harry pulled her into his arms and gave her a hug. It had been so long since someone had held her she wanted to hold onto him forever, but not because of attraction. Cash began to wonder if she'd ever really been attracted to Harry or whether she was looking at him because she was lonely. Of course he was a good friend and always would be as would David but now she began to question herself, and knew she had been lying to herself.

Cash finally pulled back and Harry released her. "You haven't hurt me. What do you mean by keeping them on their toes?"

"Come on, Cash. Surely you've seen the way those three men look at you. They eat you up with their eyes."

"They do not."

"Yeah, honey, they do. Are you sure you're not hurt and okay with who I am?" Harry asked.

"Yes," Cash answered honestly, sighing. "You'll still be my friend though, right?"

"Of course I will and so will David. You're like our little sister."

"Hey, enough with the little cracks," Cash joked, not wanting to talk about the Morten men. Harry laughed and the tension she'd seen in his face, body and eyes dissipated.

"Can't help the truth, Cash."

"You're not that much taller than I am."

"Five inches is a lot, but you're right I feel downright feminine around such big, brawny men." Harry waggled his eyebrows and they both burst into laughter. There wasn't anything effeminate about him. "David and I are going into town after work. Do you want to come with us?"

"Won't I be a third wheel?"

"You could never be that, honey, we care about you and you have barely stepped foot off this ranch in over twelve months."

"You know I don't like being around too many people."

"Yeah, but how are you ever going to end up married if you don't go out?"

"I'm not getting married."

"Cash, I know you've had a rough life, but you can't let what's in the past stop you from living in the here and now. Come on, my treat."

"If you're sure?"

"I am. We'll pick you up about eight. Is that okay?"

"Eight is good."

"Okay, see you later." Harry tugged on her ponytail and then left.

Cash wondered if she was doing the right thing agreeing to go out with Harry and David. She liked both men a lot, but the thought of being in a bar full of big, drunk men made her nervous. She would just have to make sure she stayed unobtrusive because the last thing she needed was to become noticeable in a room full of men.

She spent the rest of the day taking care of the horses and even took out one of the colts for some exercise. Although she loved to ride any horse, she liked riding the stallions the best. Fiend was her favorite mount. He was big at around eighteen hands and feisty but she and the stallion had an affinity and if she could have afforded to she would have made Clay and Johnny an offer to buy the American Quarter Horse, but Cash didn't have much money and she wasn't about to ask until she had enough to buy the stallion outright.

She'd dreamed of owning her own horse breeding operation since she was a little girl but unless things changed drastically, like winning the lottery, she couldn't see that happening in the near or even distant future.

Cashmere reined in Fiend and headed back home. The sun was already beginning to set and that meant she only had about an hour until Harry and David called to her bungalow to pick her up, and she still had to shower. By the time she got back to the yard outside the barn she was looking forward to having a night out. She'd only been to the Slick Rock Hotel once before and the food had been good, but that had been over eight months ago. It was very rare that she spent any of her free time with other people. Cash liked her alone time and spent her spare time reading. She wasn't a social butterfly and never would be but she was content. It was better to keep to herself, especially working around so many men. The only females on the Double M Ranch were Tara Morten and her daughter, who was just a toddler, but that was okay with her. Even though she and Tara were friends, Tara was busy with her children and men, which was the way it should be as far as Cash was concerned.

Pushing her thoughts aside she used the old crate to dismount from Fiend and then led him into the barn. She had already released the cinch from beneath his belly and was about to pull the saddle off when large muscular arms wrapped around her waist, lifted her from the ground and then placed her aside. She spun around to face whoever had just manhandled her and she ended up face to lower chest with a mountain of a man. Looking up into brown male eyes, she glared at him but he didn't seem to notice her ire. He turned away and removed the saddle and then the blanket from the horse.

"I'd appreciate it if you didn't pick me up like a bale of hay," Cash finally snapped. Her annoyance rose when Brutus continued to ignore her and carried the saddle out to air out on the rack and then he slung the blanket over the stall wall.

"There is nothing inanimate about you, sweet cheeks." Bruce finally faced her and eyed her body up and down. "You're all woman, sweetheart."

"My name is Cashmere or Cash," she said through clenched teeth. She took a step closer but kept her eyes on his the whole time and then she poked him in the stomach. "I would appreciate it if you would use it." She gave him another poke for good measure and had to bite her tongue when her finger bent to an unnatural angle and pain swept up it. Shit, the man was made of steel and should come with a warning label.

He just stared at her as if she were crazy and then with a shrug of his shoulders walked away. Cash growled and spun around to tend to Fiend. She worked quickly and efficiently, rubbing him down and then brushing over his coat. Giving one last check to make sure all the horses had water and feed, she hurried out of the barn. It looked like she was going to have the fastest shower on record but she wasn't backing out of tonight. She needed to get away from the ranch because the last thing she wanted was to have another encounter with the Morten men. They'd been here for a week and already they were interfering in her life. Of course she knew that Bruce had only been trying to help her but she had grown up around horses and had been taking care of the ones on this ranch pretty much on her own for the last twelve months.

Just because she was small didn't mean she couldn't handle her job. Why did men always think that women, especially vertically challenged women like her, were useless? Did they think because she was little that she wasn't capable of doing her work? The more she thought about it the more pissed off she became and by the time she stepped through the front door to her bungalow she was seething mad.

After closing and locking the door behind her she entered the bathroom, turned the shower on and stripped off. Cash was glad that she'd worn her hair up in a ponytail. Usually she would have washed it before going out, not that she did that, ever, but she didn't have time right now, and was thankful she'd washed it this morning. It should be okay after giving it a thorough brushing. As she washed, she puzzled over the way her body reacted to Bruce, Cain and Danny. Just thinking about those three big, muscular men made her breasts feel achy and her nipples began to harden. Her pussy moistened and her clit throbbed.

Why couldn't her body have reacted to Harry this way? Especially when she thought she had a crush on him? Why didn't she feel more cut up about him, now knowing that he was in a relationship with David?

Because you've been lying to yourself, girl. You made yourself believe that you wanted Harry because you knew he was safe. Her inner voice came through loud and clear and Cash thought about what her subconscious had just told her.

Had she really made herself believe she was attracted to Harry because he was such a nice, gentle, caring, loving man, and gay? Her mind whirled as she dried off and moisturized her skin. She dressed, brushed her teeth and hair and eyed herself in her bedroom mirror. All she owned were jeans, T-shirts, shirts, tanks and shorts. Of course she'd never wear shorts to work because they were totally impractical on a ranch. She would end up sunburned, and there was no way in hell she wanted any of the other hands looking at her like a woman. As far as she was concerned she was another hand like the rest of them and her femininity didn't come into it. She had never asked for or expected deferential treatment just because she was female. In fact she preferred to be treated like one of the men. Hopefully, that way none of them would look at her with anything other than respect and never with lust in their eyes.

After one last look in the mirror she pulled on her going-out boots and then grabbed her license and some cash and stuffed them in her pocket. She remembered to pick up her cell phone from the coffee table in the small living area and then went out onto the small porch to wait for Harry and David.

She was going out to dinner with friends and intended to enjoy every minute of it.

But then why did those three men keep creeping across the edge of her mind?

Chapter Two

Bruce stared toward the small cabin to the west of the house while leaning on the wooden rail and sipping from his bottle of beer. Danny was sprawled in a chair behind him and Cain was in the chair next to him. He wondered if his brothers were going to break the silence. He was still reeling with surprise at how Cashmere had been able to pick out who Danny and Cain were, since they were the spitting image of each other. Other than close family everybody had a hard time telling them apart, but not little Cashmere Woodall.

His hand clenched around the bottle until his fingers ached when he saw Cashmere come out the door to her cabin. She looked so sweet and innocent and like she was fresh from a shower. Her clothes were clean and simple but those black denim jeans showed her hips and legs off to perfection, and the red blouse set off the long curly black hair which now hung down her back. He clenched his teeth when he saw Harry and David's truck pull up near her steps. Harry got out of the truck, and after opening the back door, he lifted Cash up into the back of the truck. Jealousy swept over him and he wanted to rush over and punch the shit out of Harry for having his hands on his woman but he restrained himself. Barely.

Brutus didn't know if she had seen him and his brothers on the verandah after a long day but as David drove past the house she kept her head turned away. He followed them with his eyes and saw that Harry was looking at Cash over his shoulder and laughing. Bruce wanted to be the one to drive her places. He wanted to be able to put his hands on her body and to help her in and out of *his* truck. But she was skittish around him, he figured because of his size, and she was so little. Cashmere hardly ever looked at him, in fact she seemed to go out of her way to avoid everyone except Harry and David and he wanted to know why. Was she frightened of all men or just him in particular?

"I think we should have dinner at the hotel tonight," Cain said.

Brutus turned around to face his brothers. "Is that where they're headed?"

"Yep, I heard David and Harry talking while they were mending the fence near the corral."

Brutus tossed his bottle in the recycle bin near the end of the verandah and dug into his pocket for his keys. "Let's go."

Cain and Danny slugged down the last of their beer, tossed the bottles and hurried toward his truck, which was parked in the carport. Danny got in the back and Cain in the front. Some of the tension in Brutus's muscles released now that he knew where Cashmere was going and that he would be able to keep an eye on her. She was such a tiny thing and although she was tough and could look after herself, he felt possessive and wanted to protect her. If that was chauvinistic of him, too damn bad.

He was a man and not one of those city men who were always politically correct. Not that all the political correctness was wrong but some of it was just plain bullshit as far as he was concerned. Even governments were stepping in and banning parents from smacking their kids. He wasn't one to condone abuse in any way shape or form, but if a child needed discipline a parent should be allowed to tap their kids on the ass and not have to worry about someone coming to take their kids from them. Kids needed to learn right from wrong otherwise they could grow up to be disrespectful and get themselves in a hell of a lot of trouble.

Brutus got in the truck, buckled up and backed out of the carport. He looked in the rearview mirror and saw one of the hands looking toward Cashmere's place. He was about to stop the truck but the man turned around and walked away. Since the sun was setting and shining in his rearview mirror he couldn't see the guy's face. He would have to keep an eye out and make sure none of the men looked at Cash with lust. If he caught any of them gawking at her they would have to deal with him and his brothers.

"How do you think she could tell us apart?" Danny asked.

Brutus wondered if either of his brothers would bring up that interesting tidbit.

"I don't have a clue," Cain answered, "but I like it."

"Me too."

"She's more aware of us than she makes out." Brutus raised his voice so Danny could hear him over the radio. "She's scared of me."

"She's just a tiny little thing." Cain turned to face him and Brutus gave him a glance before turning back to the road. "She's nervous around all of us, but she's not scared of you."

"Yes she is."

"No, I don't think she is," Danny said. "We all intimidate her with our size. She doesn't even come up to your pecs, Brutus, but she's aware of all three of us."

"Do you think she'll ever give us a chance?"

"Who knows man," Cain answered. "But if I had my way she would be in my bed from tonight and that's where she'd stay."

"Don't you dare go pushing her, Cain," Danny interjected. "She's skittish enough already. We don't want her running any more than she already is."

"Shit, you know I won't do anything to hurt or upset her."

"Yes," Brutus answered. He turned on the road into Slick Rock. "We know that but Cashmere doesn't. You have to be patient. I know how hard that'll be for you but if you push her too fast you'll answer to me."

"Fuck you, Bruce."

"Calm down." Brutus pulled into a parking slot and turned off the ignition. "Danny and I know you would never hurt her, but don't go in with both pistols cocked."

"Yeah, yeah." Cain got out of the truck and headed toward the door, Brutus and Danny right behind him.

As soon as he stepped through the door to Slick Rock Hotel, he scanned the room looking for Cashmere, Harry, and David. He spotted them at a table toward the back hallway and his gut roiled with envy when he saw that she was sitting between the two men and she was laughing. God, she was so fucking sexy and had no idea how appealing she was. Her face was framed by those long black curly tresses which made her skin look creamy white and her lips were a perfect cupid's bow. Her bottom lip was full and lush and even though her top lip was thinner it was formed beautifully. He could see the flush to her cheeks even in the dim light of the room and he wanted to go over there, scoop her up into his arms and hug her tight.

He headed toward the bar with his brothers, ordered some beers and then moved toward the only table unoccupied, which also happened to be next to the one Cashmere was sitting at. She looked up and when her eyes met his, the laughter faded from her face. He cursed under his breath but didn't look away. She must have realized she was staring because she quickly lowered her gaze and her cheeks flushed. The waitress brought out their food and just as he and his brothers took their seats, she turned to take their order.

Brutus was conscious of Cashmere like he'd never been of another woman. He shifted in his seat trying to relieve the pressure on his hard dick but nothing seemed to help. He'd been walking around with a semi-hard and full-on erection since the first day he and his brothers had come to take over from his cousins and he wondered if his balls were actually turning blue. It certainly felt like it.

Bruce strained to hear what Cashmere and the two other men were talking about but made sure to keep his eyes from her. If she saw him looking she would probably become self-conscious and clam up.

"How old were you when you left home, Cash?" David asked.

"I went to live with my grandmother when I was sixteen."

"Thank God you were able to leave that place," Harry said. "Was living with your grandmother better?"

"Yes. I learned all about horses living on her ranch, but when I turned eighteen she decided to sell up and travel."

"Wow, that must have been hard on you." David took a sip of his drink.

Bruce looked at Cashmere from under his eyelashes and saw her give a slight shrug.

"She wasn't an affectionately demonstrative person, but at least she didn't hit me."

Bruce clenched his fists and his muscles went taut. He couldn't imagine someone hitting any woman or child for that matter, but especially not such a little bit of a thing. He wanted to pull her over onto his lap, wrap her in his arms and demand to know who had hurt her, and tell her that no one would ever hurt her again, and then he would go and beat the shit out of the fucker, but he had no right.

When he heard Cain growl low in his throat he looked up and saw that both his brothers were just as upset and angry as he was. He leaned over so that he wouldn't be heard. "Hold it together and just listen."

"How long did that fucker hurt you?" Harry growled the question.

"Six years."

"Jesus!" David sat back in his chair and glanced toward Bruce.

Bruce could tell by the look on David's face that he and his brothers had heard every word, but David looked back at Cash when she began talking again.

"And where was your mother? Why didn't she step in and protect you? Better yet, why didn't she pack up and take you with her?"

Bruce glanced at Cash and watched as she put another forkful of food into her mouth. The way she drew that silverware from between her lips was so sexy he nearly groaned when the image of them wrapped around his hard cock flashed into his mind. He took a deep breath and forced those thoughts away. This wasn't the time or the place and he felt a little guilty for feeling horny when she was explaining about her abusive past.

"She left when I was five years old. She was having an affair with my father's brother and one day she had a babysitter come over and I never saw her again."

"Did that asshole beat your mother, too?"

Bruce was glad that he looked at Cashmere when she answered, because her voice was so quiet he wouldn't have heard her reply, but he was able to read her lips and her answer was "yes."

"Why didn't she take you with her?"

"I don't know," Cash said and Bruce heard the hitch in her voice, "and I never will."

Harry reached across the table and took her hand. Bruce wanted to go over and remove it from his woman but he pushed his jealousy aside. She needed comfort and it didn't matter who gave it to her right now.

"Why not, honey?"

"My mother and uncle were killed by an out-of-control truck on the highway near Durango."

"So your father took his anger at your mother out on you for six long years?"

"Yes."

Harry looked at Bruce this time and he could see the muscle twitching in his jaw as he tried to contain his anger. David's voice drew his gaze and then he watched Cashmere gulp down half a glass of wine.

"How big was he?"

She glanced over to Danny and Cain and nodded her head, then leaned forward, obviously trying to keep her voice from carrying. "Their size."

Bruce couldn't take any more. The thought of a man as big as his brothers beating on her as a kid, when she would have been half of her pint size, caused rage to run through him. He pushed his chair back and headed to the bar. One of his brothers was going to have to drive the truck back to the Double M Ranch, because he was about to get shit-faced drunk. It was the only way he would be able to stay away from her.

No wonder she was so skittish around him and his brothers. They were all large men and she would no doubt do anything she could to avoid being alone with them. He ordered a whiskey and downed the shot in one go. It burned as it went down but when it hit his roiling belly some of the tension eased. He was about to order another one but he looked over his shoulder when a hand landed on his arm.

"Getting drunk isn't going to help," Danny said. "If she sees you that way you'll scare her more."

Bruce hung his head and took a deep breath. His younger brother was right. He gave a nod, scrubbed a hand over his face and finally turned around.

"Come on back to the table. Our food has arrived."

"I've lost my appetite."

"Bruce, you are going to need every bit of energy to continue working the ranch while we try and woo our woman. As much as I would like to go and find her father and hit the living shit out of him it won't change anything. What's past is over and done with. We'll take it slow with her but I'm not backing away."

"Do you think she knows we want her?"

Danny shrugged. "I'm not sure but David and Harry do. I think they got her talking so we know what we're up against."

"Yeah, you're probably right. When did you get to be so wise, little brother?"

"When I heard the pain and fear in her voice when she was talking about the man who was supposed to love and take care of her."

Bruce followed Danny back to the table. He looked at Cashmere, who was downing the contents of another glass of wine. She was obviously hurting more than she let on but he wasn't about to let her wipe herself out with alcohol. He walked up to Harry, leaned down and whispered in the man's ear.

"Don't you think she's had enough?"

Harry gave a slight nod and held up two fingers, letting him know it was only her second drink. But by the way her cheeks were flushed and the glazed look in her eyes, it was clear she was a lightweight when it came to liquor. Bruce straightened and met Cashmere's gaze. She gave him a lopsided smile, waved and then giggled. He smiled back and then sat back in his own chair and began to eat. He hardly took his eyes off of her the whole time he ate his dinner and neither did Cain or Danny. If Bruce had his way he would wrap her in cotton wool and never let her out, but he knew she would never let him or his brothers treat her like a delicate rose. Although she looked as fragile as a flower, Cashmere was tough, or so she seemed to think. But he'd seen another side of her tonight, a bruised vulnerable child hidden beneath that tough exterior and if she knew he and his brothers had heard every word she spoke tonight, he knew there would be hell to pay.

Bruce fell a little more for her and hoped that he and his brothers could convince her that she was the woman they had been waiting for. The conversation at the other table had taken on a lighter tone and he was glad to hear Cash talking passionately about her future plans to have a horse breeding program, but also to give back to the community once she was up and running by having disadvantaged and disabled kids out on the weekend for pony rides. That also confirmed his belief that their woman had a loving, nurturing nature and a heart of gold. She would make a great mother.

His sight turned inward as he imagined her belly ripe with his or his brothers' child and he was more determined than ever to keep her in his life.

Chapter Three

Danny couldn't believe how calm he appeared when inside he was so full of rage he wanted to put his fist through a wall. How the hell he had been able to talk logically and rationally to Brutus was beyond him. His muscles were so tight he was scared he was gonna snap. How he had sat there without moving or gasping for breath while she had told Harry and David what her childhood had been like he didn't know. She was no bigger than a minute now, let alone when she'd still been a young girl. How she had survived abuse at the hand of a man his size…fuck. He couldn't go there. Not here and now. If he kept thinking about it he might just lose control.

Cashmere stood up and gave a giggle when she wobbled slightly. Harry reached out and grabbed her arm to steady her.

"Where are you going, honey?"

She blinked slowly and then pushed out her lower lip. His dick twitched and he shifted as his jeans got a little tighter. "To the ladies' room."

"Okay. Do you want me to walk you to the door?"

"No." She smiled and blinked again. "I'm fine, but thanks."

Danny watched the sway of the sweetly rounded ass as she walked down the hall to the restrooms. When she disappeared from sight he turned to David and Harry but Harry beat him.

"I lied to you and to Cash."

"What about?" Bruce asked.

"I was trying to goad you all when I said I like women, too. I don't."

Danny stared at Harry a moment and then reached over and offered him his hand. "Thanks for coming clean. I feel a hell of a lot better knowing you won't be going after our woman."

"What about you, David?" Cain asked.

Danny exhaled quietly hoping that David and Harry could see his tension. He looked at his brothers and saw they were just as het up awaiting his answer.

"No, I'm not into women."

"Thank Christ for that." Danny shook David's hand, too. His brothers offered the two men their hands to let them know none of them had any hard feelings.

"You need to be careful with her." Harry gave each of them a hard stare. "She's more fragile than even she knows."

"Yeah, we got that," Danny replied, looked toward the hall and then down at his watch. Cashmere was taking her time coming back to the table. She'd been gone for nearly five minutes already.

"Does she know that all of you are attracted to her?" David queried.

Bruce shrugged and then he too glanced toward the restrooms.

"We'll take it slow with her," Cain said and looked toward the ladies room. "I like her ideas of having a horse breeding program and letting the disadvantaged ride on the weekends."

"She's a caring woman and I don't want to see her get hurt." Harry drew Danny's gaze.

"The last thing we want to do is hurt her," Danny answered.

"Cash and I have been friends from the day she started here." Harry frowned as he too looked down the dimly lit hallway. "I think of her as my little sister." He turned back to look each of them in the eye. "If you hurt her, you'll be answering to me and David."

Danny nodded and then stood. He liked that it wasn't just him and his brothers looking out for Cashmere, but right now he needed to see that she was okay. He noticed that one of the light bulbs near the rear emergency exit door at the end of the hallway had blown. That wasn't good when the women's bathroom was near the back. He would have to speak to the owner, Tyson Osborne, and make sure it was replaced. He'd met Tyson and his brothers Sam and Damon on the last visit to his cousins' ranch. Sam owned a garage and Damon was a sheriff along with Luke Sun-Walker. The three men were also in a ménage relationship with their wife Rachel. In fact the rural Colorado town, Slick Rock, was prominent for its unconventional relationships.

Just as he reached the middle of the hall he heard a soft feminine cry. He picked up his pace and hurried to the end of the hallway. He roared with rage when he saw small boot-clad feet between the spread legs of a tall muscular man and then he caught a flash of red as the woman tried to escape the bastard's clutches. Danny grabbed hold of the asshole's shirt and spun him around. His fist connected with his jaw and he was about to punch him again when a light touch halted his raised arm.

"He's out cold, Danny. Please, don't kill him."

Danny was brought out of his rage-filled haze by her sweet shaky voice and only then felt the weight of the unconscious man still in his grip. He let go of the shirt and stepped around him when he dropped to the floor. His hands were shaking as he reached out for Cash but he froze when she flinched and pushed herself tighter against the wall.

"I would never hurt you, sugar. Don't be scared of me."

"What the fuck is going on?" Bruce's loud, deep voice caused Cashmere to jump and she wrapped her arms around her waist and tried to fold in on herself. She was sliding down the wall and Danny wondered if she was fainting. He snagged her around the waist and gently pulled her into his arms and body. Her little hands clutched at his shirt and he could feel her shaking. He wanted to know what that asshole had done to her but first he needed to calm down and comfort her. Besides it was too fucking dark to see much.

Danny looked over his shoulder at Bruce's furious face and quietly began to explain what he'd seen. Cain was standing behind and slightly to the side of Bruce and he was looking angry and worried. Danny turned back to Cash and tried to ease her away so he could see if she was hurt but she just clung to him tighter. The shakes wracking her body weren't letting up and he was becoming concerned, too.

He smoothed his hand over her head and hair and down her back. "Shh, sugar you're safe. He won't hurt you again."

"What the hell is going on here?" Tyson Osborn asked as he came hurrying down the hall. Bruce stepped in and told him what Danny had seen.

"Fuck. Shit. I'm sorry guys, I had no idea that bulb had blown. It was working fine when I opened earlier today. I'll get on that right away. Is your woman okay?"

"We don't know yet," Bruce answered. "We haven't had a chance to look her over."

"Bring her to my office," Ty replied.

Danny slid his arm down to beneath Cash's knees and lifted her up into his arms. She still hid her face in his chest but he was glad to feel that she had stopped shaking. He followed Ty and his brothers back down the hall, across the room to another hallway away from the bar. Ty opened the door to his office and held it while Danny carried Cash inside. Bruce and Cain hurried in after them, as did Ty, and he closed the door. He sat on the sofa across the room but kept holding her. She shifted her body around until she was straddling his lap but she kept her face hidden from view.

"Cash, look at me sugar," Danny coaxed in a quiet voice.

She shook her head and kept her forehead pressed between his pecs. Another shudder caused her to shiver. "Come on, Cash. I need to know that you're not hurt." She gave a small whimper and shook her head again.

Cain, Bruce and Ty were all looking worried.

"Do you want me to call a doctor?" Tyson asked.

"Do you need a doctor, Cash?"

Again she just shook her head. Danny was worried sick but he was also getting frustrated. He needed to see her, but didn't want to scare her by manhandling her and forcing her to comply with his will.

Bruce moved closer and sat down beside him and Cain did the same on his other side. Danny looked over to Ty and nodded for him to give them some privacy. Ty opened the door but stopped before stepping through. "Let me know if you want a doctor sent for or anything else."

Bruce nodded but shifted his attention to Cash when Ty left. Danny hadn't stopped running his hand up and down her back, hoping his caresses would help soothe her fears.

"Look at me, sweet cheeks," Bruce demanded in a firm tone. Danny was glad his brother had kept his voice from booming out too loudly, but the tone was enough to have Cashmere obeying.

Danny sucked in his breath when he saw her right cheek was red and her eye looked swollen. She also had a fat lip and it was split and bleeding. Cain roared with fury which made Cash jump and squeal with fear and she pushed her face back into his chest and started crying.

"Fuck, Cain, good going, asshole." Danny glared at his brother but he kept his voice low and calm. Inside he was seething but not really at his twin brother. Although he was annoyed Cain had scared Cash, he knew he would never do anything to hurt her and his brother was raging just like he was inside.

"Cain, go and tell Ty to call a doctor," Bruce ordered.

"No," Cashmere said and finally lifted her head. She was a mess and Danny wanted to spend the rest of the night holding her close. His muscles were tight with anger but he made sure to keep his touch soft and gentle. The last thing Cash needed was to feel threatened by him and his brothers.

The door to the office burst open, admitting Harry and David. "How is she?"

Danny felt jealousy curl around his heart and lodge in his gut when Cashmere scrambled from his lap and ran into Harry's arms.

"Oh God, honey, I'm sorry. I should have protected you."

Danny wanted to tell Harry that it was his and his brothers' job to take care of Cash, but they hadn't done a very good job. Not when she had gotten hurt on their watch.

Cain still looked angry and jealous as he watched Cash in Harry's arms but then he mumbled to Danny. "I'm going to get her some ice and I want a doctor to check her over." He hurried out of the office.

Danny was glad that his dominant twin wasn't going to let Cashmere refuse medical treatment. He'd wanted to race her out to their truck and drive her to the clinic, but he didn't want to frighten her further, so he kept his mouth shut.

"Bring her over here." Bruce looked at Harry.

Harry gave him a nod and then leaned down to whisper into Cash's ear. Danny wanted to know what he was saying because occasionally she nodded and shook her head, but finally she eased out of Harry's hold and turned around. When he saw her bruised and swelling face and eye again, he had to concentrate on keeping his breathing calm and even. Fury pulsed in him and he wanted to go back out and punch that fucker over and over again. Even though doing so would maybe make him feel a little better, it wouldn't take away Cash's pain.

She took a hesitant step toward them and then another and another. The fifth step brought her close enough to touch, but she kept her head lowered, which brought her hair forward as if she was trying to hide from him and Bruce.

"We would never do to anything to hurt you, Cashmere," Bruce whispered. "I just want to hold you and make sure you're okay. Will you let me?"

Cash nodded but still didn't look up. Bruce slowly lifted his arm and held his hand out to her. Danny waited with bated breath to see if she would take the comfort his big brother was trying to give her.

When she raised her hand it was shaking, but then she put her little hand in Bruce's and threaded her tiny slim fingers with his thick ones. He exhaled slowly as some of the tension in his body dissipated. Cash surprised him when she next gave a sob and threw herself at Bruce.

Bruce groaned and then wrapped his arms and big frame around her. Cash rubbed the left side of her face against Bruce's chest and inhaled deeply. *Is she smelling Bruce? Does she like the way he smelled to her?* Cash reached up and wrapped her arms around Bruce's neck and sighed.

The office door opened again and the doc followed Cain inside. His brother also had a towel-wrapped ice pack in his hand.

"I would like to be alone to examine my patient." The doctor gave them all a hard stare and gleam of satisfaction shined in the man's eyes when Harry and David left, closing the door behind them.

Danny wasn't about to leave and from the scowl on Bruce's and Cain's faces they weren't either. They all needed to know that Cash was going to be alright.

"Okay." The doc sighed and then sat in the middle of the sofa next to Bruce and Cash. "These men are worried about you little lady, will you let me look at you?"

Cash nodded and then withdrew her arms from around Bruce's neck. Bruce gripped her waist and turned her on his lap so her back was to his front and she was facing the doctor. Danny and his brothers watched as the doctor took her blood pressure and listened to her heart through her shirt. When he was done he checked her face. Cash flinched but didn't make a sound as the doc examined her.

"Nothing is broken. You're going to be sore for a few days and will end up with some bruising. Ice that face as much as possible and if the pain gets any worse come and see me at the clinic. Take two pain pills every four hours for the first twenty-four hours but don't exceed the maximum dosage. Are you hurt anywhere else?"

Cash shook her head but then changed it to a nod. The doctor looked at him, Cain, and Bruce then back to Cashmere. "Would you like these three men to leave the room?"

Again she shook her head, changed it to a nod and then flinched when she bit her split swollen lip. Danny didn't want to leave the room, and by the look on his brothers' faces neither did they, but leave they would, if it meant that Cash got the medical care she needed. Bruce tightened his hold on Cash, stood with her in his arms then turned and gently seated her back on the sofa. He held the door open until Cain and Danny exited and shut the door after them. All three of them stood with their ears pressed against the door. They wanted to know where else Cash was hurt and if she was too timid to speak of it and this was the only way they would know, then so be it.

"Shit," Danny heard the doctor say. "I hope one of your men cleaned that bastard's clock for him." Danny figured Cash must have nodded because the doc said, "Good."

"You'll need to ice that, too," the doctor's voice came through the door. "It will help with the bruising. I'm going to disinfect those scratches, but it may sting a bit."

Danny moved back from the door when the doctor's footsteps came closer. He could tell by the heavy walk it wasn't Cashmere. Bruce and Cain stepped back and leaned against the hall wall with their arms crossed over their chests. The doctor's face was grim but when he turned back to say good bye to Cash, he smiled. After he closed the door he looked at each of them.

"Is she your woman, boys?"

"Not yet, but we're hoping to change that real soon," Cain stated.

The doc gave a nod. "You need to be careful with her. She's got bruising on one of her breasts where that bastard squeezed her hard and she has scratches on her lower abdomen from his nails where he tried to get into her pants."

Danny gasped and closed his eyes as his muscles bunched. He snapped them open when the doc touched his shoulder. He looked at

Bruce and saw he had his fists clenched and Cain was gritting his teeth. "She's going to be real skittish so go slow with her. Call me if you need me."

"Thanks Doc," Bruce said and then he and Cain thanked the elderly doctor, too.

Danny had taken a step toward the office door but Bruce halted him by grabbing his arm. "I don't want her going home alone tonight. I need her to stay at the ranch house with us."

"We can't force her but we can ask." Danny sighed. "If she baulks maybe we can get Harry and David to stay at her cabin with her. At least we know we can trust them not to ogle or touch her and they will look after her. If she refuses to come home with us and something happens in the night they can call us and we'll be there in minutes."

Cain stepped forward. "I'd also prefer she slept in the house with us, but your idea is good."

The three men nodded at each other and then Danny opened the door. His eyes swept the room to where Cash had been sitting on the sofa then scanned for her quickly when he didn't see her. His knees nearly buckled with relief when he saw her standing at the window staring out. She was holding the ice pack Cain had left on the desk against her face. Just as he moved toward her a knock sounded on the open door. Danny and his brothers turned to see the two sheriffs standing in the hallway.

"Can we come in and get a statement?" Luke Sun-Walker asked as he looked over to Cashmere.

Cash answered before Danny could. "Please, come in Luke, Damon."

Danny had no idea that Cash knew the sheriffs but he supposed it would be impossible not meeting them since she had lived on the outskirts of Slick Rock for nigh on twelve months.

"Are you all right, Cash?" Damon moved around Danny and closer to her.

"Yeah, I'm okay. Just a little sore."

"Why don't you sit down and tell us what happened?" Luke suggested.

Cash sighed and then gave a nod. When she was seated Luke pulled out his recorder. "Do you mind if I use this instead of writing everything down?"

"No, that's fine."

"Okay," Damon said. "Why don't you start at the beginning and tell us what happened?"

"I went to the ladies' room. When I came out it was dark and I was a little tipsy since I'd had two glasses of wine and don't normally drink." Cash drew a ragged breath and then gulped. Damon gave her an encouraging nod. "I stumbled and accidentally bumped into a man. I don't know who he was. I've never seen him before. Anyway he was obviously drunk because when he spoke he slurred his words. I apologized to him and then tried to move around him but he grabbed my arm and stopped me. I asked him to let me go but he just gave a stupid grin and grabbed my waist and spun me around.

"I was about to yell but as he pushed me up against the opposite wall he began kissing me." Cash sobbed and wiped the tears from the good side of her face. Danny sat down beside her and held her hand. Cain sat on the other side of her on the sofa and wrapped an arm around her shoulders. Cash didn't try to pull away but gave them each a small grateful smile.

"I tried to hit him, but he grabbed my wrists and held them in one hand. No matter how hard I tried to escape, he was too strong. He— He grabbed my breast and squeezed so hard I cried out, but since he was trying to shove his slimy tongue down my throat the noise was muffled."

When she shuddered and gagged at the remembered assault Danny couldn't take any more. He slid his arm around her shoulders, pushing Cain aside and then the other beneath her knees and lifted her onto his lap. Cain gave him a scowl but Danny ignored his brother.

He needed to comfort Cashmere. He ran a hand up and down her arm and hugged her side into his chest.

"I tried to get my knee up hard between his legs but I was much shorter than he was and since he had me pushed into the wall I couldn't get any leverage to get high enough. That's when he hit me in the face. He moved his hand from my breast and down to the waistband of my pants and tried to undo my jeans. He pulled my shirt up and scratched my stomach with his nails. He let go of my wrists and was pulling at the fastenings on my jeans when Danny pulled him off me."

By the time Cash was finished she was crying again. The sobs were so hard they shook her whole body. "Give her to me," Bruce demanded.

Danny looked at the rage and fear on his older brother's face and knew if he didn't get to hold Cash in his arms again that he would lose the tight rein of control he had himself under.

"Cash, Bruce wants to hold you, sugar. He needs to know you're safe. Will you let him?" Danny kissed her head and hugged her. Her tears finally slowed and then she nodded. Danny passed her off to Bruce and watched as his big brother shuddered as he cradled her against his chest. Cash wrapped her arms around his neck and nuzzled her nose into his throat.

Luke cleared his throat, drawing Danny's gaze. "Tell me what you saw and did?"

By the time Danny had finished giving his statement he felt weary to the bone, but he was also pent up and knew he would have a hell of a time sleeping that night. He was going to see that fucker attacking Cash over and over in his nightmares. Danny was just glad he got to her before she got hurt worse.

"I'll be out sometime tomorrow with your typed-up statements so you can sign them." Luke nodded toward Cash. "Take your woman home, she's been through hell and is exhausted."

"She's asleep," Bruce said quietly.

Danny held the office door open for Bruce as he carried Cash and then looked at Cain. "Bring the truck up close to the back. We'll go out one of the emergency exits so we don't wake her up going through the noisy bar."

Cain gave Cash a look of longing before nodding and hurried away. Danny caught the door his brother had left through so it wouldn't slam shut and held it wide as Bruce carried her out.

Hopefully Cash was out for the night and they could have her sleep in their home where she would be safe.

Chapter Four

Cash groaned at the ache in her eye and cheek but she was so warm and comfortable she didn't want to move. When she did move her leg it connected with something hard and warm. She tried to open her eyes but it felt like they were glued shut. One eyelid cooperated but the other refused. The events of the previous night came rushing back and she sat up with a gasp. She looked around at the strange bedroom and then down the bed next to her when the mattress dipped.

Bruce was in bed next to her, his brown eyes watching her. She gulped when she realized his chest was naked and hoped the rest of him wasn't. His chest was so thick with muscles she could see every delineated line when he moved. He shifted and leaned up on his elbow with his head resting on his hand.

"How are you feeling, sweet cheeks?"

"Okay. Where am I?"

"At the ranch house."

"Why am I here?"

"You fell asleep, Cash, and I wanted to make sure you were safe. So I brought you here."

"Umm…" Cash looked down to see a huge T-shirt covering her chest. When she shifted she sighed with relief when she felt she still had her panties and bra on. Thank God he hadn't seen her totally naked. *As good as,* her inner voice said, which caused her to shiver. Did he like what he'd seen or was he turned off? *Why are you even thinking that way, girl? He's just taking care of you because you work for his cousins.*

She reached up and brushed the hair from her face, gasped and winced when her hand connected with her swollen eye and cheek. Bruce rolled out of bed and she couldn't help but stare at his godlike body. He was ripped and cut and bulged everywhere but she was glad to see he had on a pair of boxers. He bent down and picked his jeans up from the floor, which made the knit material of his underwear stretch over his muscular beefy ass. She wanted to crawl over the bed and take a bite out of it. Heat shot up her face when he turned around to face her. He smiled and gave her a wink as if he knew she had been ogling his backside.

"I'll get you some painkillers, sweet cheeks."

"Why do you call me that?"

The smile on his face widened and he waggled his eyebrows, "Because you have the sweetest little peach of an ass I've ever seen."

More heat swept into her face and she felt like it was on fire. He bellowed out a laugh, winked at her again, and then turned toward the door. "Feel free to have a shower if you want, sweetie. You can wear another of my T-shirts when you come out." Bruce pointed to the dresser drawer where she could find his shirts and then left.

Cash couldn't believe how turned on she was, especially since she'd thought herself in love with Harry. God was she so fickle? Why did she have to be lusting after three men who were way out of her depths? Her breasts were swollen and aching and not because of last night. Although she still had a little pain where that asshole had grabbed her, the ache she was experiencing right now was different. Her nipples were hard, her clit was throbbing and her pussy was wet. She was going to have to go home and shower there instead of using this one, because she didn't have any clean underwear with her and she wasn't about to put wet undies back on.

She knew they owned their own ranch and wondered why they were taking such good care of her. But she figured that because she was their cousins' employee that they would feel guilty if anything happened to her whilst they were looking after the Double M Ranch.

Cash winced as she got out of bed and stood up. The skin on her face felt tight and so did her eye. She also had a headache but she'd dealt with worse and she had work to do. Thank God it was Saturday and she only had to work a half day, and tomorrow she would spend the day resting in her cabin with a good book. Looking around the room, she spotted her jeans and red blouse on the chair near the door and her boots were placed neatly on the floor below. She didn't want to put her shirt back on but she stepped into her jeans, dropped her red shirt on the floor and found her socks in her boots. After she put them and her boots on she picked up her blouse and headed out.

The delicious scent of cooking food wafted to her nose and she inhaled deeply, but by the look of the light shining through the living room window she was already late for work, so she headed to the door and had her hand on the handle.

"Where do you think you're going?"

Cash screamed, jumped, and spun around all at once. She placed a hand on her rapidly beating heart and tried to gain her breath.

"Sorry, baby." Cain moved closer. "I didn't mean to scare you. I brought you the painkillers." He held up his hands and showed her two pain pills in his palm and a glass of water in the other.

"Thanks." She took the medicine and drank down the water.

"So, where were you going?" Cain nodded toward the door.

"Work."

Cain shook his head, reached out and took the shirt from her hand and then gently gripped her arms with his free one. "Not happening, baby. The doctor's orders were to rest and that's exactly what you're going to do."

"I'm fine, Cain."

Cain took another step closer and nudged her chin up. "No you're not. I can see the pain lines around your lips, and from the tension in your forehead you have a headache."

"I've had worse."

"Jesus, Cash. Stop arguing with me, you aren't working and that's final. Now come on into the kitchen, breakfast is ready."

Cash couldn't hide the shiver that ran down her spine when he dropped his hand to her shoulder and caressed down her arm. The huge T-shirt she was wearing was falling off and in danger of exposing the top of her breast through the neck hole. Before she could adjust it Cain stroked a finger over her collar bone and down to the material of the shirt. She shivered again and then felt her flesh goose bump. Cain had been watching his finger as he caressed her and seemed to snap out of his trance. When he looked at her she could see the hunger in his eyes. She went to lower her head but he stopped her with a finger under her chin and gazed at her intently.

"We would never do anything to hurt you, baby. Do you trust us?"

Cash gave a slight nod.

"Good." Cain didn't give her a chance to speak because he moved quickly. He stepped into her until their bodies were touching, wrapped an arm around her waist, and lowered his head. He gently brushed his lips back and forth over hers and she was surprised that his lips were so soft, and she figured that just maybe he was being careful with her because of her fat lip. Cain could be such a hard-ass and she had expected him to kiss hard, too, but he kept his touch light. Tingles of warmth began to travel through her body, making her feel weak and feminine and even though her body liked it, her mind didn't.

Just as she placed her hands on his chest to push him away he lifted his head and released her. "Breakfast is getting cold." He took her hand again and led her toward the kitchen.

Bruce and Danny were already just sitting down to eat. There were platters of bacon, scrambled eggs, toast and pancakes. She'd never seen so much food for only four people and wondered if some of the ranch hands were joining them.

Cain seated her to Bruce's left where he sat at the head of the table and then sat down beside her. Danny was sitting across from her. There were four mugs of coffee on the table as well as cream and sugar, maple syrup and jars of jelly. The men began loading their plates and when they had finished all eyes were on her. Bruce sighed and then reached over and picked up her plate. He had two pieces of bacon on her plate already and was about to put another on, but she stopped him.

"That's more than enough, thank you. I don't eat as much as you three do. I'm not as big as you are."

Bruce gave her a look but then he scooped up some eggs and finally put a piece of toast on her plate. He quirked an eyebrow and pointed at the pancakes and she shook her head. He put the plate in front of her and then starting eating. Cash sighed because even though she wasn't very hungry she knew that these three domineering men weren't going to let her get away without having breakfast.

Everyone was silent as they did justice to the meal and by the time Cash had eaten her fill, her plate was still half-full. She'd never been one to eat breakfast often and didn't know how she was going to do her work on such a full stomach. That was another thing. Cain had demanded that she rest but other than being a little achy around her cheek, her swollen eye, and the slight headache, she was fine. She had no intention of letting them dictate to her. She was going to do her job and that was all there was to it.

"You didn't eat enough, baby." Cain's gravelly voice drew her eyes. "How the hell are you going to heal if you don't fuel up?"

"I'm fine, Cain." She sighed and then took a sip of her coffee.

"Don't give me that shit," Cain snapped. "Do you think we can't see that you're in pain? God you are stubborn."

"Pot, kettle," Cash snapped back.

Cash watched with amazement as the scowl on Cain's face turned to a grin and then he rasped out a deep belly laugh. A smile tugged at her mouth but she was determined to hold her glare. There was no way in hell she was going to laugh with him even if his humor was catching.

Bruce reached over and covered the hand she had resting on the table. "You're just full of surprises aren't you, sweet cheeks?" He was grinning and the smile lit up his whole face. God, they were all so handsome and her body kept taking notice. If she didn't get out of here soon she was going to do something she would regret.

She removed her hand from beneath Bruce's and gathered her dirty dishes and rose, intending to take them over to the kitchen.

"What are you doing?" Danny asked.

Cash hesitated and rolled her eyes. She looked back over her shoulder. "I'm going to rinse my dishes and then I'm going home to shower where I'll have some clean clothes to put on."

"And then you're going to rest, right?" Cain ordered more than asked.

"Yes, Cain," Cash lied.

"Good," Bruce said. "I don't want to see you back at work until at least Wednesday."

She ignored him and took her dishes to the kitchen, rinsed them, put them in the dishwasher and then headed out. She paused in the doorway and glanced back over her shoulder only to find all three sets of eyes pinned to her ass. Clearing her throat to get their attention, they each let their gazes peruse her body until they met hers. Her breath hitched in her throat when she saw the hunger there. Heat suffused her cheeks but she wasn't about to acknowledge what she saw in their eyes. "Thank you all for taking care of me."

She didn't wait for a reply but lit out of there as if her pants were on fire, because they were. By the time she got back to her cabin her panties were so wet they were uncomfortable. She hurried to the bathroom, showered, dried off and dressed. After brushing her teeth and drying then braiding her hair, she headed to the barn.

Cash had been working solidly for over an hour, mucking out stables, laying fresh hay and then making sure the horses had plenty of water. She had just picked up the bucket holding the grooming tools when the door burst open. Harry and David came rushing in and they looked worried.

"What's wrong?"

"You're in a heap of trouble, Cash."

Fear skittered down her spine but she had no idea what she'd done wrong. The two men looked scared for her, which caused her heartbeat to race, and when they stopped before her she realized she was panting for breath.

"What's going on?"

"Cain went over to your cabin to check on you. He's headed this way. You might want to run."

"Oh shit." Cash covered her mouth with a shaking hand.

Harry and David burst out laughing and their humor turned her fear to anger. They had made her think something was terribly wrong. She didn't appreciate their sense of humor. Just as she was about to give them a dressing down, she caught movement near the open barn doors and saw Cain coming toward her.

He looked madder than a disturbed hornet's nest.

"This should be fun," David snickered. She shot him a dirty look.

"Cash," Cain roared. "What the fuck do you think you're doing?"

Each step he took brought him closer and closer. His body was taut with anger and his fists were clenched. Cash backed up with each step he took and she dropped the bucket of brushes when her back collided with a wooden stall wall. When he raised his hand she whimpered and dropped to the floor. She curled up into a little ball and covered her head.

* * * *

Cain was so damn mad he was shaking. He'd gone over to check on Cash and had become worried when she hadn't opened the door to her cabin when he knocked. When he tried the door and found it unlocked he walked inside worried that she was in pain and couldn't come to the door. When he found the place empty and that she hadn't locked up, raged consumed him. He spun around slamming out of her place and headed toward the barn. He spied David and Harry fixing one of the wood slats on the corral near the barn and Harry looked up and gave him a wave. Cain was too pissed off to acknowledge him and picked up his pace.

Harry and David dropped what they were doing and went racing into the barn, no doubt to warn Cash that he was on the warpath. Those two had been told last night that Cash wouldn't be working today and they had promised to take over her chores. They must have seen her sneaking into the barn and now were trying to warn her.

Moments later he was storming into the barn, and his fury got the better of him when he saw that the stalls had already been mucked out and fresh hay put down. Cash had just picked up the bucket of grooming tools but she had done more than enough as far as he was concerned.

"Cash," Cain roared. "What the fuck do you think you're doing?"

She looked up at him and started backing away. That only pissed him off more. When she bumped into the wall and couldn't go any further he lifted his arm, intending to take the bucket from her hand.

Cash dropped the bucket, whimpered and then fell to the ground and before he knew what was going on she had curled up into the fetal position with her arms over her head.

Fuck! Way to go asshole. She thinks because you're angry that you're going to hit her. After hearing about her childhood last night and then her getting hit, you shoulda known better.

Harry took a step and was in a half-crouch position when Cain gripped his shoulder and stopped him. "Let me take care of this," Cain said in a quiet voice. "Keep everyone out of here." Harry nodded and then he and David walked out.

Cain sighed over his insensitivity but Cash was going to have to learn that just because he or his brothers got angry sometimes, didn't mean that they would ever hurt her. He knelt down and scooped her up into his arms and carried her over to a bale of hay and sat down. She was still making whimpering noises and he could feel her shaking.

"Baby, Bruce, Danny, and me would never hurt you." He kept his voice low and hopefully soothing. She was still curled up on his lap with her hands protecting her head. "Cash, I would never raise my hand to you. Come on, honey, don't be scared of me. I'm sorry. I didn't mean to scare you."

Her shaking slowed and then stopped and she lowered her arms. She peeked up at him and then she tried to sit up. Cain helped her until she was sitting upright with her side against his chest and her legs hanging off his. She felt so damn right in his arms he didn't want to let her go.

"Sorry." Cash's breath hitched and she lowered her head.

Cain placed a knuckle beneath her chin and nudged her face up. "You have nothing to be sorry for, sugar. I guess your reaction was instinctual, huh? I was going to take the bucket from you, not hit you."

Cash looked at him with a blank expression for a moment and then her eyes widened. Red swept up her neck and into her cheeks. She pushed at the arm he had around her waist but he wasn't about to let her go. Not now that he had her where he wanted her. She pushed at his arm again and when he didn't let go she dug her short nails into his forearm.

"Let me go," she whispered.

"Why?"

"Because I asked you to," Cash yelled.

Cain sighed but removed his arm. She scrambled from his lap and paced away and then spun around to face him. He looked up when he saw Bruce and Danny entering but Cash was so intent on him she didn't hear his brothers stop behind her. Bruce raised a questioning eyebrow but Cain ignored him and focused back on Cash when she pointed at him.

"I can't believe you. You and your sanctimonious brothers heard every word I said last night, didn't you?"

"Yes," Cain answered honestly and then watched with horror as tears filled her eyes.

"Oh God," Cash sobbed. Turning blindly, she plowed right into Brutus. She gave a startled cry and then looked up at his big brother.

Bruce wrapped his arms around her waist to steady her and Cash surprised him once again by bursting into tears. She hid her face in Bruce's torso and hugged his big body. Bruce stroked her back and made murmuring noises until she was finished with her crying. Instead of letting her go as Cain expected, Bruce gripped her waist and lifted her up until her head was level with his shoulders. Cash placed her hands on his shoulder for balance and then wrapped her legs around his waist. God, she looked so tiny against Bruce's hulking body. Cain wanted to pull her from his brother's arms and have her wrap him that way. He was getting a little jealous of the way she seemed more connected with Danny and Bruce. He wondered if she was scared of him because of his harder attitude. Well, he wasn't changing for her so she was going to have to learn to get used to it. Besides, Danny and Bruce could be just as arrogant and dominant as he could. Even though Bruce was the quietest out of the three of them and slower to react, if his big brother was pushed too far, then there was hell to pay. He nearly smiled when he imagined their tiny woman going toe-to-toe with Bruce. He pushed his thoughts away when Bruce began to talk.

"What's going on in here, Cash? Why were you crying?"

Cash lowered her head and tucked it beneath Bruce's chin. It looked like she was going to be stubborn. Cain stood, moved in close to Cash's back, and rubbed soothing circles between her shoulder blades, explaining what had happened. All the time he talked he kept his eyes on her bent head. She peeked up at him and stared daggers at him.

"If you weren't already hurt I would spank your ass for looking at me with attitude like that."

Her jaw dropped open and then she closed her mouth, pulling her lips tight.

"I think it's time we talked," Danny said and Cash blanched as if she hadn't realized Danny was there.

"Good idea, brother." Bruce began to carry Cash out of the barn. "It's beyond time."

Cain followed his brother and their woman to the ranch house. He just hoped like hell that they could convince Cash to give them a chance. But after what she'd been through with her childhood and again last night, he wasn't sure how she was going to deal with what they wanted from her.

Chapter Five

Bruce and his brothers had thought about selling up their ranch near Alamosa four and half hours away and relocating their operation to this area when they'd heard about the polyandrous relationships in Slick Rock. Now that they had found the woman he could see having in his life for the rest of his days he wanted to start the ball rolling. But first things first.

He loved the way Cashmere felt in in his arms and against his body last night as he cuddled up with her and again now with the way she clung to his neck. He didn't want to let her go but he knew she wouldn't put up with being carried for long. She was trying to hide from Cain, Danny and him right now, but he didn't think it was because she was scared of his brother. Cash may have reacted to Cain's anger initially, but now she was calm, he thought she might be embarrassed over her reaction. And the fact that she now knew they had heard her talking to David and Harry about her abusive childhood.

After Cash had left the house this morning he and his brothers had talked about how much they wanted her in their lives. But first she had to learn that when they said something they meant it, especially when her health and welfare were at stake. Bruce didn't stop until he entered the living room and sat on the sofa and when he tried to pick Cash up to set her on the cushion next to him she tightened her arms around his neck.

"What's going on with you, sweet cheeks?" He kept his voice low so he wouldn't startle her. "Come on now, Cash, my brothers and I want to talk to you." She clung tighter and shook her head no.

Cain looked worried and he knew his brother was still beating himself up for scaring her, but by the determined gleam in his eyes he wasn't going to let her get away with hiding from and ignoring them. Bruce decided she needed to see he could be just as indomitable as Cain. He reached up and gently pried her hands from behind his neck, nodded to Cain to help him and between the two of them, placed her on the sofa. Cain sat on her other side and Danny sat on the floor in front of her, crossing his legs so he could get closer to her.

"Cashmere, look at me," Cain demanded. Bruce watched as her spine straightened, her shoulders pushed back and finally she lifted her head. "I'm sorry I frightened you, honey. Yes I was angry to find that you had disobeyed us and gone to work, but don't ever think that I would raise my hand to you." Cain stroked a finger down her uninjured cheek. "When I get upset I'm likely to yell, but I would *never*, *ever* hit you."

"Yet, you told me you'd spank me. You lied!"

"No, I didn't." Cain scrubbed a hand over his face and sighed. "Don't you know the difference between someone beating on you compared to an erotic spanking?"

Bruce heard her slight gasp and dropped his eyes to her chest. Her nipples hardened and pushed against the front of her shirt in turgid little points. She shifted on her seat and squeezed her legs together.

Is she imagining herself over Cain's lap while he spanks her?

"You know that Slick Rock is full of ménage families, don't you?" Danny asked.

Cash turned to face him and nervously licked her lips. "Yes."

"Haven't you seen the way the men interact with their women? How they pamper them and treat them like queens but how protective they are of their wives?"

"Look, I don't get out much and I haven't really had much to do with anyone except for my bosses and Tara, and even then only minimally. She's busy looking after her kids and her men."

"Do you think Tara is happy with her life?" Cain asked.

"She's so much in love she glows," Cash replied, even it if it was a little pithily.

"She does, doesn't she?" Bruce didn't expect an answer. But the question he was about to ask he wanted an answer for. "Why do you think that is, Cash?"

"How the hell should I know?"

Danny got up onto his knees and placed his hand on hers. "Do you think it's because they satisfy her in bed? Or maybe it's the way they make sure she takes care of herself, making her eat when she should and rest when she's tired or not feeling well?"

"She could be happy because she has two men seeing to her needs, making sure she finds pleasure in their arms before they find their own," Cain said. "Or because there is always one of them around to help her out with the kids."

"I think it's all those things," Bruce said, drawing Cash's gaze. "But I also think it's because they love each other very much and can lean on the others when they need to. A relationship isn't all give, Cash. It takes a lot of work to keep things on an even keel. Sex is a big part of it but unless there is a bond of friendship and everyone is willing to compromise and communicate then I don't think it would survive."

"Why are you telling me all this? What has any of this got to do with me?"

"We're attracted to you, Cashmere, and we want what our cousins have with Tara, with you." In the silence that followed Bruce's declaration, he could have heard a pin drop. Cash opened her mouth and then snapped it closed again. She glared at him and then turned her scowl onto his brothers. He wanted her to tell him yes but from the look in her eyes that wasn't about to happen.

"No!"

Bruce's chest ached but he'd be damned before he showed any vulnerability in front of her by trying to rub the pain away.

"Why the hell not?" Cain asked. "We know you're attracted to us, baby. Why are you denying the connection between us?"

Cash's body tightened as if she was getting ready to bolt and Bruce wasn't about to let her. She needed to rest and he was going to see to it that she did. Her hand lifted to her temple and she rubbed it with her fingertips, massaging in little circles and besides her bruising her face was paler than normal. She was in pain but was too stubborn to say or do anything about it.

"I'm never going to get into a relationship and get married," Cash blurted in a half shout.

Those words told Bruce how much her momma leaving and then her father's abuse had affected her. He was going to have to sit down and come up with a way to get around her worries, but for now he was going to make her take a nap.

"We'll talk more about this later, sweet cheeks." Bruce stood up and held out his hand to help her from the sofa. "You are going to have a nap." When she stared at his hand and then looked up at him he raised his eyebrow. That action seemed to let her know he wasn't about to back down. "I'll walk you to your cabin, Cash, but if I see you anywhere on the ranch other than taking in the sun on your porch or sitting under a tree reading a book I will put you over my lap and smack that ass when you've recovered. Are we clear on that?"

"Crystal!" Cash said through clenched teeth, taking Bruce's hand. When she was on her feet she pulled her hand free and headed for the door. "Don't bother seeing me out, I'm a big girl and don't need your help."

Bruce watched her hips sway as she stormed out of the house. Their woman was a little spit fire when she had a mad on. He couldn't wait until she unleashed that passion on him and his brothers in the bedroom, or the living room, or maybe the kitchen table. He groaned and shifted his hard cock trying to get a little more room and then headed to the kitchen for some coffee. Cain and Danny followed him and sat down at the table, lost in their own thoughts until the fresh pot of coffee finished brewing.

Cain was the first one to break the silence as they sipped their drinks. "I can't believe I scared her after what we heard last night. Fuck!" He thumped his fist down on the table with self-castigation.

Bruce couldn't let his younger brother keep thinking that way or he was going to back off and ruin everything. "I don't think she's scared of you, or us, Cain. Her reaction was understandable considering the abuse she got from her father."

"How can…"

"Let me finish," Bruce interrupted. "Yes, she's scared, but of herself, not of us. You saw the way she clung to me, trying to hide from you. If she was frightened of us she wouldn't have done that."

"What…"

Bruce held up his hand, "I haven't finished. Cash said she's not interested in a relationship or marriage, correct?"

His brothers nodded in agreement. "She never said anything about sex." He paused to watch their reactions and they didn't disappoint. Cain and Danny both sat up straighter in their chairs and waited for him to continue. "When we were talking about our cousins and Tara, especially the intimate parts, she was squirming. The thought of having more than one man touching her got her aroused. Her nipples peaked and she was squeezing her thighs together."

"Where are you going with this?" Danny asked, showing his impatience.

"What if we offer her all the sex she wants?"

A wicked gleam formed in his brothers' eyes.

"I figure if we can get her into bed and keep her satisfied that the rest will follow. She's not the type of woman to have sex with just anyone. If she agrees then we know that she has a least some feelings for us and we can build on that. Hopefully we can touch her heart and end up with what we want from her. In our beds and lives, *permanently.*"

"We need to move the ranch," Cain blurted. "You both heard what she said about breeding horses and the kids?"

Bruce and Danny nodded.

"We talked about having one woman to share between us but didn't see how we could make it work until Clay and Johnny told us about their relationship and the ménages in Slick Rock." Cain paused to take a breath.

"Go on," Bruce encouraged. He already had a fair idea where Cain was heading.

"Polyandrous families are accepted here. They wouldn't be where we live and I don't want Cash having to deal with slander that could come her way if she was involved with us. We have great ranch hands that are already trustworthy looking after our place while we're here and I asked them a few months back if they would be willing to relocate with us if we moved."

"What was their answer?" Bruce asked eagerly.

"They had no problems with it. They're all single and aren't in serious relationships, or weren't at the time anyway. We can pay out anyone if they don't want to come along but I don't think that will happen. If we asked I know they would pack everything up and move the whole shebang."

"That's a good plan," Danny said. "But we can't expect our hands to pack up our house and all the animals. It wouldn't be fair to them. We're going to need to put the ranch up for sale and it could take time to sell in this economic climate."

"Wait," Bruce interjected. "We're getting ahead of ourselves. We need to get Cash into our lives first. When that looks like it's working out then we can start on the ranch. But I will call a few estate agents tomorrow and get some valuations. So are you in, boys?"

"I think that just might work." Danny smiled.

"I'm in," Cain rasped as he adjusted his crotch.

"Then let's start planning how to get what we want," Bruce said.

* * * *

Cash threw herself onto the bed and hugged the pillow to her chest. Her body was achy and she didn't know what to do about it. Those three men got her aroused just by breathing, but the way they made her feel was so out of the norm for her it scared her. When they were talking about their cousins satisfying their wife she had imagined those three men touching and kissing her naked body. It had been hard to concentrate on what they were saying but when Bruce had said they wanted that with her...Well she'd just about melted into a puddle on the floor.

How the hell she was going to get through the next few weeks seeing them around the ranch and keeping them at arm's length she had no clue, but she was determined to succeed. She'd seen what marriage did to people and didn't want a bar of it. When her mother had left her father he had taken to drinking and become bitter and mean. There was no way she was letting anyone do that to her. Bruises and injuries healed but once a heart was broken it stayed that way. She wasn't going to put herself up for that kind of pain.

Cash sighed and tried to clear her tumultuous mind. She was actually thankful that Bruce had put his foot down and ordered her to rest. Her head, cheek and eye were throbbing like a bitch. Her body relaxed and she let herself drift into sleep.

Bruce held her hips while Cain and Danny removed her clothes. When she was standing naked in front of them she felt vulnerable and exposed but she was so hungry for their touch that it overrode her anxiety. Bruce's massive warm body was against her back and he smoothed his big manly hands up her sides as if taking in her shape through touch. Cain had her eyes pinned with his and no matter how hard she tried she couldn't look away. He intimidated her a little with his forceful personality and attitude, but those traits also seemed to make the fire smoldering inside her burn hotter. She didn't know how much more she could stand before she begged the three sexy, hot men to make love to her.

Cain moved closer and cupped her face between his hands. She felt like she was drowning in those intense pools of hazel. He slowly lowered his head and she stopped breathing in anticipation, and as his lips got closer to hers she reached up and gripped his wrists. She loved the feel of his skin and muscles under her hands and fingers and wondered what it would be like to run them over his chest and stomach. He brushed his lips over hers, back and forth as if waiting for something. She sighed and her lips parted. Cain licked her lower lip and she couldn't help but moan with desire. He thrust his tongue into her mouth and glided it along hers. She loved his taste and copied his moves, trying to get more. Two large warm hands cupped her breasts and she cried out into Cain's mouth as he explored every part of her.

When her nipples were squeezed between fingers and thumbs she arched her chest, hoping they wouldn't pull away. Pleasure zinged from her breasts to her pussy, making her internal muscles clench as cream dripped out. Her clit was throbbing with need and felt swollen between her legs.

Cain lifted his head and then scooped her up into his arms and carried her over to the bed. He placed her into the middle of the mattress and got on beside her. The bed dipped on the other side and when she turned her head Danny bent forward and started kissing her. His kiss was hot, wild, demanding, and carnal and left her wanting more.

Hands caressed her legs, rubbing up and down her shins until they reached her knees. They gently nudged her thighs apart and she didn't even think about protesting. She wanted this more than her next breath. Fingers lightly trailed up the inside of her inner thighs, stroking and teasing, going higher and higher. A large hand cupped her mound and she sobbed with pleasure at the pressure on her needy clit and bucked up into the touch.

"You like it when we touch you, don't you sweet cheeks?" Bruce asked and his breath caressed her wet folds, causing her to shiver.

"Yes. Please," she begged.

"Please, what sugar?" Danny asked and then began kissing his way down her neck.

"Touch me."

"We are touching you, baby," Cain said just before he leaned down and sucked her nipple into his mouth.

"More, please? I need more."

Cash looked down when Bruce swept his fingers through her slit. She was so wet they slid through her folds with ease. He scooted off the end of the bed, grasped her around the ankles and pulled her toward him, pushed her legs wide and without any warning he lowered his mouth to her pussy. She cried out as he licked and nibbled at her labia and then his tongue rimmed around her hole. Her hips began to rock without conscious thought and then she mewled as he laved over her clit. Again and again he swiped over the engorged pearl until her body was shaking. Heat swept through her from the inside out until she felt like she was about to go up in flames. Two hot mouths latched onto her nipples and suckled strongly. A finger began to push into her tight wet cunt and pleasure assailed her. The walls of her pussy gathered in, growing tauter and tauter, but just as she was reaching for whatever was on the other side of her pleasurable torment, a loud bang sounded.

Cash gasped for breath and looked down to see that she was clutching the pillow with one arm and her other hand was between her legs. She was hot, sweaty and achy but she didn't know what to do about it. She jumped when another thump sounded and she realized someone was knocking on her door. Running a shaky hand over her hair, hoping it hadn't come loose from the braid, she rolled off the bed and went to see who it was.

"Hi, Cash." Arty Cannon, one of the ranch hands, stood outside with his hat in his hand and a nervous smile on his face.

"Hi."

Arty looked away and she could see his face was a bit red and he scuffed his boot on the wooden deck before meeting her eyes again. "I was wondering if you wanted to come out to the hotel for a drink with me."

"Uh, thanks for the offer Arty, but I've had enough of that place for a while."

Arty gulped and looked down again but he looked kind of angry. Cash took a step back and put her hand on the door ready to close it, but when he met her eyes again his face was expressionless. "Yeah, I heard about that. Are you okay?"

"I'm fine, but thanks."

"I'll see you around then."

"Yeah," Cash replied and quietly closed the door. She'd never seen Arty looking at her with interest, before. Surely he hadn't been asking her out because he was attracted to her? No, he was probably just being nice after hearing about that guy attacking her. Cash had made damn sure that none of the men looked at her in a sexual way and as far as she knew none of them had. She treated them like they were her brothers and they treated her like any other hand, or so she had thought, except for her temporary bosses, of course.

She groaned as the dream flashed back into her mind and headed for the bathroom. It looked like she was going to be taking more showers than usual. Maybe she should start washing her panties out while she showered. At the rate she was going through them, she would run out of underwear before she did her laundry.

Chapter Six

Bruce hadn't seen Cash since Saturday and he was hankering for a sight of her. He was feeling a little anxious and wanted to be able to hold her in his arms, but he was just grateful she had spent the whole of Sunday resting in her cabin. Harry and David had visited her on Sunday afternoon and when Cain had seen them coming out of her place, he had grilled the two men on her condition.

What worried him was that Harry and David said she seemed a bit distracted and nervous. He supposed she would be jumpy after being attacked and confused after what he and his brothers had told her, how they wanted to have a relationship with her. Was she worried about having the attention of three men instead of just one? They hadn't really asked her how she felt about what they wanted from her. But her emphatic denial still had his guts in knots.

It was Monday morning and Bruce wondered if Cashmere was going to be a good girl and continue to rest up, or if she was going to push their boundaries and work. Bruce hoped that she decided to head to work. He would let her do her chores until lunchtime but then he was going to move in on her. Imagining his hands caressing all over her petite naked body had him groaning, shifting on his feet and adjusting the fit of his jeans. She was the sexiest woman he'd ever seen and knew she was the one and only woman for him and his brothers. Convincing Cash was another story. He glanced toward her cabin as he stood on the porch sipping his coffee. The sun wasn't up yet but he could see a light on in her place.

The door to her cabin opened and there she stood silhouetted in the shining light behind her. He could tell she was dressed in jeans, shirt, and boots, ready for another day on the ranch. Since she couldn't see him, as he'd left the porch lights off, he smiled and mentally rubbed his hands together. If she was feeling well enough to work maybe she would be well enough to feel his hand on that peach of an ass. In his mind's eye, he had her lying naked over his lap with her ass in the air. He would run his hands on those sweet cheeks and when she was relaxed he would apply his palm to her backside. Would she moan and thrust up into his touch or would she buck and fight him? Either way he knew she would be aroused. He and his brothers knew how to turn a woman on with an erotic spanking. By the time he finished with her she would be begging for him to fuck her.

Bruce moved his hard dick to the side because the metal zipper was making him uncomfortable. Just as Cash disappeared into the barn his brothers came out onto the verandah.

"Cash just went into the barn."

"What?" Cain snarled. "God, that woman is a piece of work. We told her not to come back to work until Wednesday. I'm going to carry her…"

"Wait a minute," Bruce said when Cain turned toward the steps but halted when he spoke. "Let her go for now."

"But…" Danny began.

"No, she can work until lunchtime. She's an independent woman and needs to feel in control, but"—Bruce paused—"we touch her every opportunity we get so she gets used to being near us. We are so much bigger than her, since she's just a tiny little thing. Plus we bring her here for lunch and make sure she rests for the rest of the day. I'm going to have a word with David so that someone takes over her and our chores this afternoon. Since he's foreman there should be no problems there."

"Do you really think this is going to work?" Danny asked.

"We can only hope," Bruce replied, "but we do everything we can to woo her. Hopefully after giving her as much sex as she wants she won't be able to do without us. That beautiful woman is already attracted to us and has feelings that she is in denial over. The sooner we start on courting her the sooner we ensnare her."

Danny and Cain nodded and smiled. Bruce could see they were eager to get started and so was he. He only hoped their plan didn't backfire on them and sent her running in the opposite direction. It was a big risk, but one he was willing to take, because Cashmere was one of those women who loved once and deeply. That was one of the reasons she hadn't dated anyone. He and his brothers had asked Harry and David a lot of questions about her over the last week and a bit, and thankfully they had answered with what they knew. The other night listening to her talking to the two men had been another eye opener and even though Bruce was still angry over the way her father had treated her, learning what he had had also given him more information on her personality and how to deal with her.

No one else would dare touch her or look at her with lust in their eyes, at least not while he and his brothers were around. He didn't have any qualms whatsoever about letting everyone know that she was theirs and once she was in their arms, he was never letting her go.

* * * *

Cash had only been in the barn for ten minutes when Arty came in. When she looked over to see him watching her, she smiled at him and then continued on with her chores. As the silence continued she began to feel a little uncomfortable and creeped out, so she turned to face Arty.

"Did you need something, Arty?"

"No." Arty continued to stare at her with a vague blank look, and tendrils of uncertainty ran up her spine. She looked away but then met his gaze again. He cleared his throat and began to speak. "Do you need some help?"

"No." Cash sighed. "Thanks anyway, but I'm sure you have enough of your own work to do."

Arty nodded but didn't look like he was going to leave. Cash turned her back on him and got back to work. When she glanced over her shoulder again she sagged with relief. Arty was gone.

What the hell was that all about?

Cash was mucking out the second stall when Danny entered the barn. She was about to scoop up another shovelful of soiled straw but stopped when he came up behind her. She stiffened and wondered if he was going to tell her off because she was supposed to be resting, according to him and his overbearing brothers, but waited without saying anything.

She inhaled deeply when his arms came around her waist and he moved into her until his front was against her back. The heat emanating from him was turning her on, that and the fact that he had his hands on her. One hand was gripping her hip, his thumb stroking over her hip bone through her jeans and the other was splayed wide over her lower belly. The tip of one of his fingers was so close to her mound. Her clit began to throb and juices leaked out.

"Hi sugar, how are you feeling?"

"Good," she answered breathily.

Danny leaned down, nuzzled against her neck and breathed in, "You smell good, Cash. Good enough to eat." He licked her neck and then nipped her earlobe.

Cash shifted her feet closer and pressed her thighs together, but it didn't help relieve her aching clit at all. In fact, it only made the ache worse. Just as she thought about doing something stupid, like turning around and kissing him, he released her and stepped away. She took a minute or two to get her breath back and to shore up her defenses to try and hide the way he had her body reacting, and turned around. He wasn't there. Glancing to every corner and back toward the door, she didn't sight him. How the hell he had left without her hearing him she had no idea. Now that he was gone she felt...a little cold and maybe even bereft.

She didn't understand why she was feeling this way since only last week she thought she had a crush on Harry. Was she so fickle that she didn't know her own heart and mind? It seemed so. With a sigh, she pushed her confusion aside and got back to work. There were still another twenty stalls to be cleaned and then she had to fill the horse's water troughs and set the food out into buckets for later that afternoon. With her still feeling a little sore in the face and with her bad eye only able to open partially, it was going to take her a lot longer than it usually did to get through it all.

* * * *

How could she let that man touch her when she knew she belonged to him? He wanted to go and punch that fucker out for putting his hands on her, but if he did he would lose his job and he wouldn't be able to see her any more. She was such a gorgeous, sexy woman and even though she wouldn't go out with him, he had seen the way she looked him over and knew she wanted him just as bad as he wanted her. But she was shy and would never do anything to look like a slut. Cashmere Woodall was as pure as fresh snowfall and wouldn't let any man touch her until she was married. He was going to be that man. He'd spent the last three months making plans and he wasn't about to let the Morten cousins ruin everything.

He slipped back into the shadows of the tack room when one of the other Morten's entered the barn. It was easy to get in and out of the barn without anyone being aware of his presence. Four of the wooden boards on the back of the tack room wall had come loose near the ground and all he had to do was lift them up and squeeze through the hole. He always made sure no one was about when he slipped through. It wouldn't do for anyone else to know how to get close to his woman without being seen.

Fury consumed him when the other Morten touched his betrothed. He wanted to go get his rifle and shoot them all, and then he wouldn't have to worry about them touching his wife. Cashmere was the optimal virgin bride and such a hard worker. She never had a bad word to say about anyone, not even those gay assholes David and Harry. Even though he hated the foreman and his partner they had done a good job of protecting his woman, so if he ended up taking anyone out, it wouldn't be them.

He was such a generous, handsome man. His momma told him so. She also told him he could have any woman he wanted. Well, he wanted Cashmere Woodall and he was going to have her. No matter what he had to do to achieve his goal, she would be his.

Of that he was certain.

* * * *

Cain watched as Cash dumped another shovelful of manure into the wheel barrow. She was looking a bit tired and he wanted to order her back to the house, but he would follow Bruce's plan for now. When she sighed and leaned on the shovel handle he pushed away from the wall and walked toward her. As he got closer he noticed that her face was pale and she looked like she was in pain. Whether she had seen him moving from the corner of her eye or heard him move he wasn't sure, but she looked over her shoulder, connected with his eyes for a moment, and then looked down at the dirt floor. He stopped only a step away from her and she slowly looked up, but as she did her eyes wandered over his body.

Oh yeah, Cain said to himself as he watched her body respond to his nearness. *You're more interested than you let on, aren't you, baby? I hope you like what you're seeing because you're going to be seeing a hell of lot more very, very soon.*

"How are you doing, baby? Do you want some help?"

"I'm good," she said. "This is the last stall and then I only have the water troughs to fill and the feed buckets to set out."

"Hmm," Cain murmured. "Well, when you've filled the troughs, could you come up to the house? My brothers and I would like to talk with you."

"Umm, okay."

Cain took the last step which brought him close to her and wrapped an arm around her shoulder and pulled her into him. She rested her forehead against him and slumped for a moment but then she must have realized what she was doing and pulled away. He wanted to take the shovel from her hands, fling it aside, pick her up and carry her to the house, and then he would strip her down and put her into bed and order her to rest. Cashmere Woodall was so damn stubborn and would keep going until she fell down. She needed someone to take care of her and that was going to be him and his brothers.

"Don't work too hard, Cash," he said in a firm voice and although he could see her getting irate with his order, there was also longing in her eyes as she gazed toward the barn door. Cash was struggling and if he and his brothers didn't keep a watch on her she was going to get sick. He wasn't about to let that happen. Striding from the barn quickly he went in search of Bruce. It was time for big brother to put his foot down and take control. He'd been walking around on eggshells with Cash, but that had to change. Bruce needed to step up to the plate and be the man he really was. Of course they were all going to have to step carefully, but it was time to up the ante, especially if they wanted to keep Cashmere in their lives for good.

* * * *

Bruce was itching to go into the barn, sling Cash over his shoulder and carry her into the house, especially after Cain had told him that she was struggling. Even though he admired her tenacity, everybody had a limit and it sounded like Cash was reaching hers. He knew she'd had to be stubborn and resolute, otherwise she may not have survived, but everyone needed a helping hand, someone to lean on now and then and he suspected Cash had never had that. She had been virtually on her own since her mother had left her at the age of five and all she'd learned was that she was only good as a punching bag to her father and a slave to her grandmother. But she hadn't backed down or given up and had come out of her childhood with a dream still intact and the skills to go about getting that dream. He wanted to be able to help her achieve that goal, but one step at a time.

It had been half an hour since Cain had spoken to him and Bruce figured that was more than enough time for her to finish up. There wasn't any way he was letting her groom all those horses and then feed them. If he'd had his way she would have spent the day in bed recuperating.

When he entered the barn he didn't first see her because it took time for his eyes to adjust from the bright sunshine to the dim interior. When he did, his heart stopped in his chest and fear skittered up his spine. He rushed over to her, where she was slumped on the floor against a bale of hay. It looked like she had been dragging the hay across the dirt floor. Her face was so white she looked like a ghost, and her eyes were closed. He placed a finger against her neck and sighed with relief when he felt her pulse. She seemed to be breathing okay, deep and steady.

"Cain, Danny," Bruce roared loud enough to be heard on the far reaches of the ranch. He knew they were out in the corral next to the barn, helping some hand replace the rotting wood, and would hear him. His brothers came running into the barn and stopped when they saw him cradling Cash.

"What happened?" Cain asked.

"Is she hurt?" Danny questioned.

"No, I think she just overdid it and fainted, but I want you to call for the doctor, Danny. I want her checked out. Cain, go and pull the covers back on my bed. Since our woman can't take care of herself we're going to have to do it for her. She is going to be moving into the house for the time being and into my bed, where she'll be under our watch twenty-four seven."

Bruce had been looking over Cash while he spoke to his brothers. He'd carefully placed her on the floor so she was flat but on her side in case she got sick. His hands held her head gently and he searched her scalp with his fingertips looking for lumps in case she had whacked her head on something when she passed out. He sighed with relief when he didn't find anything.

"Give me your shirt, Danny," he said and was glad his brother had heard him since he was already on his cell phone to the clinic. Danny ripped the shirt open one-handed and then cradled the cell between his shoulder and cheek while he pulled first one sleeve and then the other off.

Bruce grabbed the shirt and wadded it up as best he could using one hand, and then slipped it beneath Cash's head. Then he lowered it gently and began to run his hands up and down her body, checking for injuries. When he couldn't find anything he picked her up and began carrying her toward the house. He was so mad at her right now. How the hell could she have pushed herself until she passed out? Why didn't she come to him or one of his brothers when she knew she couldn't do anymore?

Danny walked with him and finally disconnected the call. "Doc's on his way."

Bruce nodded toward the back door and Danny rushed forward to hold it open. He didn't stop until he was in his bedroom and then gently put her on the mattress. Cain had been waiting for them and immediately moved closer and helped by removing one of her boots, Danny did the other. Between the three of them they had her stripped down to her underwear and in one of Bruce's T-shirts in minutes. He covered her up and sat on the edge of the bed.

Danny and Cain were standing at the foot of the bed staring at her. Cain looked up and met his eyes.

"No more work for her, until she gets the all clear from the doc," Cain said in a growly voice.

"Agreed."

As he reached back to brush some loose strands of hair from her face, he heard a knock on the door. Danny went to let the doctor in.

"What's going on?" the doc asked as he entered the room. The man's lips tightened when Bruce explained how he'd found Cash. She was so exhausted she didn't stir while the doctor examined her. When he was done he nodded toward the door and left the room.

Bruce, Cain and Danny followed him out to the kitchen. "As far as I can tell there isn't anything wrong that rest won't fix. No working for at least a week. I want her back in my office Monday next week for another checkup. I think she just pushed herself too hard today and her body rebelled."

"Thanks Doc." Bruce offered his hand with gratitude and they shook. "I appreciate you coming out. Do you want a drink?"

"No, thanks, I have a few other patients to visit before heading back to the clinic. I'll set up an appointment for your woman when I get back and I'll get my secretary to give you a call with the time."

Cain and Danny saw the doctor out, but Bruce was still feeling antsy and wanted to be with Cashmere. He hurried back down the hall and was just in time to see her open her eyes. She blinked a few times and looked around the room and then frowned as if confused.

Bruce moved further into the room and then sat next to her hip. She looked so damn beautiful and yet so vulnerable. He wanted to wrap her up in his arms and tell her that he would keep her safe and love her until his last breath. But she wasn't ready to hear any of that yet.

"How did I get here?"

"You don't remember?"

"No." She sighed and then reached up and flipped her braid over her shoulder.

Bruce wanted to release her hair from its confines and see it haloed around her stunning face.

"You overdid it and fainted. I found you passed out on the floor of the barn." He took her hand in his and held it. Seeing her lightly tanned palm and fingers in his huge one showed him just how delicate she really was, although Cash would never admit to that. Not in a million years.

"This has to stop, sweet cheeks. The doctor came out and checked you over and since you pushed yourself before you were healed, you aren't allowed to work until after you've seen him, next Monday."

"But I have to…"

"Enough," Bruce commanded loudly, for once not tempering his voice. "You are going to heed the doctor's orders and we are going to see that you don't do anything more than go to the bathroom or get a drink. Do you understand? And you will be moving in here where we can keep an eye on you."

Cash didn't answer verbally but her defiant, anger-shooting gaze and her body language said everything. Bruce knew he and his brothers were going to have a fight on their hands and he could hardly wait. Cashmere was full of passion she was hiding from them but also herself. He couldn't wait for her to lose control and see the hungry desire she had burning in her eyes for real.

Bring it on, sweet cheeks!

Chapter Seven

Cash spent the next week resting, since she had no choice in the matter and even if she didn't admit it to them, the rest had done her good. She felt so much better, with more energy, and was actually looking forward to getting back to work. But she still had the weekend to get through and after she had seen the doctor Monday morning she would get back into a regular routine.

She was currently in the kitchen brewing a pot of coffee and the men were outside working where they had been all morning. Cash had decided to make herself useful and had already made lunch of stew and dumplings for when they all came inside. All the swelling had gone down and she only now had a few mottled bruises on her eye and face and she was so pent up, ready to get back to work, she couldn't settle. Bruce, Cain and Danny were probably going to have a fit at her for cooking for them but she didn't care, she needed to feel useful now that she was healed.

Footsteps sounded in the hallway and she took a deep breath as she pulled some mugs down from the cupboard and began pouring the coffee. The table was set with silverware and all that was left to do was serve the food and carry it across to the dining area. As she placed the coffee pot back on the warming plate, hard, thick muscular arms wrapped around her waist.

"What have you been up to, sweet cheeks?" Bruce's voice was so deep and manly she couldn't help but shiver in reaction when he spoke. Her body reacted to all three men as if she was in tune with them, but she had no idea how to go about relieving the ache their presence caused. But it wasn't just their presence that got her body responding with desire, if she was honest with herself. Even just thinking about them caused her breasts to ache and her pussy to moisten.

"I made lunch," she was finally able to answer after taking a deep breath.

"Something smells good, baby, but are you sure you're up to doing all this?" Cain's voice came close to her and she turned her head to the left to find him leaning against the counter with his back toward it. He was watching her through narrowed eyes as if trying to gauge her every little reaction.

She looked up and over her shoulder and met Bruce's gaze. "If you'll let me go then I can bring everything over to the table."

Bruce released her waist, but instead of stepping back like she expected him to, he placed his large, manly hands on her shoulders and turned her around. Lucky for her she hadn't picked up any of the cups yet, otherwise she might have dropped them when she saw the hunger in his eyes. He gripped her hips, and his hands were so big they nearly met in the middle of her lower back. He caressed her hip bones with his thumbs. She wondered what he was doing but she had her answer before she could voice her question. He moved his hands to her waist and then lifted her up without seeming to strain. His strength turned her on, making her feel petite and feminine. She clutched at his shoulders for balance, a little uncomfortable with her legs dangling in midair. He turned and then took two steps and lowered her to the other counter on her ass. He was so freaking huge he still towered over her, but then he bent, moving closer, nudging her knees with his hip.

Cash automatically separated her legs and then had to widen them even more when he stepped between them. He bent down until his forehead was pressing against hers and it wasn't until then that she realized she was panting for breath. "I can't hold off with you anymore, sweet cheeks. I can't wait another moment." Bruce's eyes left hers and drifted down to her mouth. She gasped but then she sighed when his lips met hers. His lips were soft but firm. He used his mouth to entice and then when liquid warmth began to travel through her blood stream, her body softened, but she was also het up with excitement.

His tongue slid over her the seam of her mouth and she grabbed onto his shirt when she swayed toward him. She'd been fantasizing about what he and his brothers tasted like over the last week and a half and couldn't stop the moan from escaping her mouth when he slanted his mouth over hers and deepened the kiss. The sound was muffled when he pushed his tongue in and slid it along hers. He ate at her mouth as if he was starving and she responded without thought. Liquid fire traveled through her veins, making her breasts ache and her pussy throb. She was so needy and knew only Bruce, Cain and Danny could quench the flames.

Bruce eased the kiss back from rapaciousness until he was sipping at her lips, and then he finally lifted his head. He was breathing as heavily as she and when a hand touched her knee, she looked up into Cain's hazel eyes. The muscles in his face were tight and at first she thought he was angry but then she saw the heat blazing out at her and knew he was very turned on.

Bruce stroked a finger down her nose and then he moved away. Cain immediately took his brother's place between her thighs and she shivered when his hands landed on her upper legs and he began to rub his palms up and down over her jeans. He didn't say anything but kept his eyes connected to hers as he lowered his head. When their lips met she was shocked at how he ate at her mouth so hungrily. Cash moaned and Cain responded with a deep growl as he thrust his tongue into her mouth. The kiss was wild, hot, wet, and uninhibited. The more he devoured her mouth the needier she became. She gasped when he drew her tongue into his mouth and sucked on it. She felt so boneless and yet so full of tension she didn't know what to do.

Cash lifted her hands and gripped his forearms and felt the steel of his muscles beneath his warm skin. She wanted so much more. That small taste of touch was nowhere near enough to appease the burning ache inside her. When he moved his arms she released them and groaned as he held her hips and pulled her closer toward him. She could feel the hot, hard ridge of his erection against her pussy even through her jeans and began to rock against him, trying to assuage the throb deep inside.

"My turn, brother." Cash was only vaguely aware of Danny's voice close by and then sighed with disappointment when Cain lifted his mouth from hers before moving back from her. She gave a squeak of surprise when Danny stepped forward and scooped her up into his arms. He shifted her until her front was plastered against his and his hands were gripping her ass cheeks, holding her up. She wrapped her arms around his neck and her legs around his waist for stability, and then looked into his hazel eyes. Danny's eyes had more green than brown, whereas Cain's seemed to be an even mix of both colors. She felt like she was drowning in his gaze. He moved so fast her vision blurred and he slammed his mouth over hers. His tongue shoved into her mouth, glided along hers and then swirled around exploring every niche of her interior.

A hard, warm chest connected with her back and huge masculine hands moved between her and Danny's stomach. They pulled her shirt out from where they were tucked in and then a hand splayed wide over her belly. The muscles beneath her skin quivered and cream dripped from her clenching pussy onto her already wet panties. Danny released her mouth and lifted his head. She was pleased to note she wasn't the only one breathing heavily.

The fingers against her stomach flexed and then caressed her, causing her flesh to erupt in goose bumps.

"So fucking soft." Bruce's deep voice caused her to shudder in reaction as his low cadence washed over her. "I can't wait to feel all of you, sweet cheeks."

Cash's breathed hitched in her throat as her mind went into a whirl. *Is that what I really want? Do I want to have his hands on my naked body? Yes! I want all of them touching me, kissing me, making love to me. Wait! Love! I don't love them. I haven't known them long enough.*

"Don't you want that too, Cashmere?" Danny asked.

She exhaled and looked up into his eyes again. *Yes.* She screamed in her mind.

"Thank God." Bruce groaned.

"Bring her to the table," Cain said in a deep growly voice.

"Wait!" Cash moved her hands to Danny's shoulders and dug her nails into his shirt-covered skin.

"What's wrong, baby?" Cain asked when Danny carried her closer.

"D—Did I...say that out loud?"

"You sure did, sugar." Danny kissed the top of her head and then bent down and placed her ass on the sturdy timber dining table.

Bruce came over and cupped her chin in his hand. "We want you, Cash. We're going to make you feel real good, sweet cheeks."

"Oh God."

Danny reached for her shirt but he must have been too impatient to undo all the buttons because he grabbed the hem and lifted it up and pulled it from her arms and over her head.

"Fucking perfect," Cain rasped and she looked up to find him staring at her breasts. Cash looked down and cursed that she had worn one of her lace push-up bras. They made her look more well-endowed than she really was and she wondered if they would be disappointed when it was gone.

Bruce reached out and with a flick of his fingers he opened the front clasp of her bra. She made a grab for the cups when they loosened but Danny, who had moved around the other side of the table, reached out, slid his hands down her arms, and then lifted them above her head. He clasped her wrists in his hands and then pulled gently, so that she began to fall back across the table. Cain placed an arm across her upper back and slowed her backward motion so she didn't hurt herself. Her chest rose and fell with each gasp she took and her belly quivered when she felt Bruce's fingers at the button of her jeans.

"I can smell your honey from here, Cash. I can't wait to get a taste of your cream."

"What are you doing to me?" she cried out.

Cash turned her head toward Cain when he got up on the table beside her. He was lying right next to her, with his head propped up on his hand. His free hand landed on her belly and then he began to lightly rub up and down on her skin. His hand crept up higher as he lowered his head. She closed her eyes just before his lips covered hers and his hand covered her breast.

Cash sobbed with overwhelming pleasure while Cain kissed her deeply, hungrily, all the while he kneaded her breast. She cried out when his finger pinched her nipple and couldn't help the instinct to arch up into his touch. Her whole body was one big aching mass of need and she didn't know what to do to stop the pleasurable pain.

Fingers tugged at her jean's button and zipper and then her ass was lifted and then jeans and panties were being pulled down her legs. Cash shivered as the cool air caressed her naked flesh. A chair scraped over the tile floor and then her legs were being pushed apart. Warm, moist air wafted over her wet pussy and then she moaned into Cain's mouth as a hot tongue licked up through her folds.

Danny released her hands at the same time Cain removed his lips from her mouth and then they each placed an arm down by her sides. Danny was still leaning over her from behind but since he was so tall he had no trouble reaching her. He leaned down and licked over the tip of her nipple and when he sucked the peak into his mouth, Cain did the same with the other. Two hot wet mouths suckling on her breasts and another licking at her pussy was almost too much to bear.

When Bruce rimmed her cunt with a large, thick finger and licked across her clit at the same time, she groaned at the pleasure and wondered how much more she could take. Her muscles were taut with tension, yet she felt so boneless she knew if she tried to stand she would fall in a heap on the floor.

Cash groaned when the tip of Bruce's finger penetrated her wet sheath and she tried to arch her hips up in silent demand for more. Two big hands landed on her belly, one up high near her ribs and the other down low so the fingers were touching her mound.

"You taste so fucking good, Cash. I want to hear you scream my name when you come."

Cash moaned. Bruce had only lifted his mouth from her pussy enough to talk and the vibrations of his voice sent more pleasure wracking through her sex. Even her ass felt the vibrations and she gasped at the unexpectedly carnal delight. Another gush of juice leaked out and covered her pucker. She was so hot and turned on, the ache inside her was interminable and she wanted relief, now.

She groaned with pleasure when Bruce's finger pushed into her pussy further and then he began to slowly retreat. Cain and Danny continued to lick and suck her breasts, sending electrical sparks straight down to her pussy until she thought she was going to go out of her mind with need.

"Please," she sobbed with pleasure and frustration.

"Please what, sugar," Danny mumbled around her nipple and she arched her chest up.

"I need…"

Cain released her nipple with a pop and then asked, "What do you need, baby?"

"I—I don't…I…need…"

Cash winced when Bruce pushed his finger into her a little deeper and then sighed with relief as he drew back. His tongue laved over her clit faster and faster and he continued to thrust his finger into her, but shallower this time. She knew that there was something she needed to tell them, but she couldn't think. Every time the words came to her lips, they drifted away on a sea of arousal as they touched her.

The fit of Bruce's finger got tighter and it took her a moment to realize he'd pressed two fingers into her pussy. She'd seen how long and thick his fingers were and just imagining what they looked like pumping in and out of her vagina sent the fire inside her burning hotter. The pressure on her clit and inside her got more intense when Bruce caged her clit between his teeth and then suckled continuously. She writhed beneath their pleasurable ministrations but couldn't move much with the hands holding her down.

She'd never felt anything like this before. It felt like her insides were being wound up tighter and tighter, like a spring was being primed and the added friction of those big fingers moving in and out of her was too much. Her legs trembled and then she screamed Bruce's name as the coil broke. Her body convulsed, fire consumed her and her pussy clenched down hard on the fingers still moving in and out of her sheath. Fluid dripped from her pussy and waves of pure rapture washed over her again and again. Her mind became fuzzy and she gasped for breath and then her head banged down onto the table when she slumped.

Cash hadn't even realized she'd lifted her head until it connected with the wood again but she was still so wrapped up in awe and wonderment that she didn't feel any pain. A chair scraped and she realized her eyes were closed. When she opened them she saw three sets of hungry eyes looked at her with what she could only describe as reverence.

"You are so fucking sexy, Cash. I can't wait to make love to you. Will you let us, sweet cheeks?"

Chapter Eight

Bruce held his breath while he waited for Cash to answer him. Her face was still flushed from her orgasm. Her long wavy hair was a dark halo around her beautiful face and he wondered which of his brothers had released it from its ponytail. If he had to hazard a guess he would guess Cain. Even though all of them loved long hair on women, Cain was more obsessed than he and Danny.

He was about to ask Cash his question again but she nodded and then looked away from him when her face turned an even pinker hue. He rose to his feet, placed his hands on the table on either side of her chest and was leaning down to kiss her when a hard knock on the front door froze him. He moved quickly when another knock landed on the wood door.

"Just a minute," Bruce yelled and lifted Cash from the table. Between him and his brothers they had her dressed in moments and then he passed her over to Cain and headed to answer the door. He looked back over his shoulder to see Cain had Cash seated and Danny was walking over to the coffee pot. There was no way in hell Bruce was letting any but him and his brothers see their woman naked. He was just glad that the kitchen window had tinted UV film over it and no one could see in. He hadn't even thought about the windows when he'd let his lust take over.

When he opened the front door to find Harry and David on the doorstep he wanted to tell them to take a hike, but he couldn't do that. David was ranch foreman and if something was wrong he and his brothers needed to know about it.

"What's up?"

"Can we come in?" Harry glanced to David and then back to him. He looked kind of nervous and angry, which was unusual for Harry.

Bruce stepped back and swept out a welcoming arm and after closing the door led the way to the kitchen. When Harry spotted Cash he rushed over and pulled her from her chair and into his arms. If he hadn't known there wasn't anything sexual in the act Harry would have had his knuckles in his mouth by now.

"You're looking so much better, honey. The week off has done wonders for you." Harry finally released Cash and kissed her on the head.

"Geez, thanks. I think."

"He's right." David hugged her and then nudged her chin up. "The tension lines around your mouth and eyes are gone. In fact you look like you're glowing."

Cash's cheeks turned red and she sat back down and wrapped her hands around the coffee mug Danny placed in front of her. When everyone else had drinks and were seated Bruce decided to get the ball rolling.

"What's the problem?"

Harry glanced at David, then to Cash, back to him and down to his mug. He could see the other man was trying to decide if he should voice what he wanted to in front of Cash, but then he sighed and then he met his gaze again.

"Some of the tack has been tampered with. One of the hands went for a ride yesterday and almost came off with the cinch broke. When he investigated it looked like it had been cut along the underside of the strap, not all the way through so that it would be noticed but a blade of some kind was definitely used on the leather. Joe came back and showed me and David so we went and checked everything that was still in the tack room. All of it needs to be replaced."

"Fuck," Cain yelled and slammed his mug onto the table. "Who the hell would want to do something like that? Someone could get seriously injured or even killed."

"Any idea if someone has a grudge against my cousins or any of the hands?" Bruce asked.

"Not that I'm aware of," Harry replied. "Everyone has worked here for years and there has never been a problem. Except for when Tara was first on the scene. The boss's ex-girlfriend took exception to their interest in their wife, but Celia's long gone."

"Hmm." Danny rubbed a hand over his chin. "So let's assume that Clay and Johnny don't have any enemies. That would mean someone doesn't like having us around."

Bruce sat up straighter in his chair. "I think you're onto something, Dan. Someone is out to make trouble for us but who?"

"What about that guy who assaulted me at the hotel?" Cash asked.

"Nah, I don't think so, sugar," Danny answered. "He was a coward and after the beating Cain gave him I don't think he'll be back. Besides he's still waiting for his court hearing and Luke and Damon have been keeping an eye on him."

"Alert everyone you have complete trust in to keep an eye out for any suspicious behavior," Bruce said. "You know the men better than we do. And send someone to get some new tack."

David and Harry rose to their feet. Harry walked closer to Cash, leaned down and whispered something in her ear. Bruce watched her face turn red and wanted to know what Harry had said, but he didn't think either one of them would tell him. Cain saw the two men out and was back a few moments later.

"Any ideas why someone would have it in for us?" Cain asked as he sat down again.

"Not a clue," Danny answered.

Bruce had an idea but wasn't about to voice it in front of Cash. If he was right, knowing what he did about her, she would blame herself. He had a feeling that someone didn't like the way he and his brothers were getting close to her. He'd seen a couple of the hands staring at Cash's body. She had of course been totally oblivious since she wasn't a femme fatale and had no clue at how appealingly sexy she was. He was going to have to word his brothers as well as Harry and David up, to keep an eye in her. The last thing he wanted was some other guy making moves on her. As far as he was concerned, she was theirs. She just didn't know it yet.

* * * *

Danny was so damned horny he didn't think he could stand it much longer. He still had the image of Cash spread out on the table naked, the way she looked and sounded when she came. Even though he was glad Harry and David had come to them with the problem, he cursed their timing. He wanted to pick her up, carry her to the bedroom, strip her naked, and bury his cock into that tight wet pussy. His dick had gone down to half-mast, thank God, but just smelling her delectable scent when she moved made it come roaring back to life.

If he was sure of her reaction, the minute Harry and David had left he would have scooped her up and made a run for it. But since they had gone Cash had kept her head down and not met any of their gazes. He would have loved to have known what was going through her head but he knew she wasn't ready to open up with them right now. And from the astonished look on his brother's face when Bruce had had his fingers inside that pretty little cunt, he had a feeling that Cash was still a virgin. He wouldn't be able to clarify that until he and his brothers had a chance to talk without prying ears around.

"When can I go back to work?" Cash asked, drawing Danny from his introspection.

"Not until you get the all clear from the doc," Bruce answered.

Cash stood up and practically stomped over to the phone. She dialed and then she was talking.

"Hi, it's Cashmere Woodall. I'd like to make an appointment to see the doctor as soon as possible please."

Danny bit back a grin. Their little woman could be so damn feisty. He loved that about her. Shit! *Love? Surely...Oh geez, no wonder I want her so bad.*

"Half an hour is fine. Thanks, see you then." Cash hung up the phone and turned to face him and his brothers and arched a brow. "Satisfied?"

"Nowhere close," Danny muttered and then glanced at his brothers when they snickered. He looked up to see a confused look on Cash's face and knew she hadn't heard him. *Thank God.*

"Let me drive you." Bruce rose to his feet.

"No, there's no need. I can drive myself or get a lift with whoever's going to town for new tack."

Bruce gave her a stare that would normally set grown men to quivering, but not their little Cash. No. She stood there with a determined glare of her own and when Bruce gave a slight nod Danny saw the relief in her eyes. Looked like he and his brothers had gotten to her and now she was going to try and keep them at arm's length again.

Not happening, sugar. We've only just begun.

* * * *

Cash gave a sigh of relief as she walked out of the doctor's office. She'd been given the all clear and was hankering to get back to work. She made her way toward the supply store where Harry was getting new tack and as she walked along she glanced into the shop windows. When she spied a red dress on a mannequin she stopped to admire it. She didn't own any dresses and the sight of it called to her. After glancing around to make sure no one was watching her she entered the store.

Looking in the mirror of the dressing room, Cash eyed the stranger staring back at her. She looked pretty even without any makeup or heels on, and the material was so soft and made her feel sexy as it slid over her skin when she moved. Having no idea whether she would get a chance to wear the dress didn't really matter. There was a yearning inside her to have that dress. *Would Bruce, Cain and Danny like it? Would they think she looked sexy with it on?* What did it matter? She had no intention of getting with them again. She'd made a huge mistake letting them make love to her the way they had. Cash was only setting herself up for a fall.

She took the dress off with every intention of placing it back on the rack, but minutes later she left the store with the red dress and matching shoes in a shopping bag and went to meet Harry.

He was just coming out of the store when she got to his truck.

"All set?"

"Yeah."

"So what did you buy?" Harry asked and glanced from the road toward her, nodding at the bag on her lap.

"Nothing."

"You don't have to hide from me, Cash. I know you care for them."

"I don't."

"You keep telling yourself that honey and you may eventually wind up believing it."

"I can't, Harry."

Harry slowed the truck and then pulled over onto the shoulder of the road and turned the truck off.

"Everyone has scars, Cash. You can't let the past stop you from living. We all get hurt at one time or another but you can't live your life on what-ifs."

"They are so domineering and arrogant."

"Yeah, but they're hot," Harry said. "Imagine what it'd be like to have those three sexy hunks at your beck and call, three men to touch and love you. What if they are the loves of your life and you throw that away because you're scared?"

"But…"

"I never figured you to be a coward, honey."

Cash looked out the front window of the truck. *Is Harry right? Am I a coward?*

"They love you, Cash. I can see it in their eyes."

"But what if you're wrong?"

"What if I'm not?" Harry reached over and gripped her chin, making her meet his eyes. "Are you willing to throw away something that could be special because you're afraid of getting hurt?"

Harry released her chin and shifted so he was facing her. "I was so damn scared of telling my family I was gay, Cash. I knew if my father found out he wouldn't accept that part of me but I had to be true to myself. So, one day I finally gathered up the courage to tell him." Harry sighed and ran his fingers through his hair. "My mom already knew but we'd kept it a secret. I couldn't go on living like that anymore. I felt like I was betraying my dad, so I manned up and told him. Well, you should have seen the disgust in his eyes. He never once looked at me again. He told me to pack up my stuff and get out. It cut me to the quick knowing I would never see my mom and dad again, but do you know what?"

Cash shook her head.

"I felt like a huge weight had been lifted from my shoulders. Telling my dad was freeing. It let me accept who I was deep inside. It didn't matter what he thought, it didn't change who I was inside. I left without a backward glance and traveled until I wound up here and here is where I met the love of my life. I still keep in touch with my mom by phone and email and hopefully one day my dad will see the light and accept me, but David is the most important person in my world and I wouldn't change a damn thing."

He snatched the shopping bag off her lap and peered inside. Then he reached in and pulled the dress out and held it up. After whistling through his teeth he put the dress back into the bag and handed it back to her. Harry shifted around until he faced the front again and then started the truck. Neither of them said anything until they were almost home.

"So, when are you going to get into that sexy dress you bought?"

"I'm not sure," Cash replied.

"But will you wear it?" Cash knew that Harry was asking so much more than that simple question. He wanted to know if she had the courage to go and get what she wanted.

"Yes, I'll wear it, *eventually*."

"Good girl."

Harry dropped her off outside her cabin and she raced inside to hang up her new dress. There was no need for the three Morten cousins to know she had been thinking about them. She was looking forward to getting back into a normal work routine. The hard work aided her ability to think clearly. Now that she knew she was going to give Bruce, Cain, and Danny a chance she had to figure out a way to go about it. She had no women friends she could call on for advice, and although she was sure David and Harry would be delighted to help, she wanted to do this on her own. Just thinking about trying to seduce them made her shiver and caused goose bumps to erupt all over her body. She'd had a taste of their love making and wasn't sure she'd survive the real deal, but it was going to be a hell of a lot of fun trying. Those three men packed one hell of a wallop and the thought of them making love to her all at the same time got her juices flowing, but now wasn't the time to be thinking about such things. She had work to do.

Cash froze when she saw the flower on her pillow. Someone had been in her home. She glanced around but didn't see anything out of place until her eyes snagged on a partially open dresser drawer. She pulled it open and covered her hand with her mouth. Nestled on top of her bras and panties was a white sheet of paper which had letters pasted onto it.

YOU'RE MINE

IF YOU DON'T WANT ANYTHING TO HAPPEN TO THEM STAY AWAY

A shudder of fear worked up her spine and she felt violated, almost dirty, knowing that someone had seen and probably touched her underwear. Bile rose in her throat but she swallowed convulsively until the sick feeling left. Her first thought was to pick up the paper and show her men, but then she wondered if she did that if she would be putting them in more danger. Grabbing a pair of panties to use so she wouldn't put any fingerprints on the paper, she picked it up and carried it into the kitchen and placed it in an empty drawer and then slammed it shut.

Racing back to the bedroom she scooped up all her underwear and took it to the small washing machine off the kitchen. After loading the washing and turning it on, she pressed start. Cash didn't really want to wear any of that stuff again, but she didn't have much money and there was no way she could afford to go out and buy all new stuff, especially after her splurge on that dress.

Grabbing the key from the nail beside the front door she locked up before heading out to work for the rest of the afternoon. She thought about taking the dress and the shoes back to the store for a refund but quickly vetoed that idea. She'd never owned anything sexy and there was no way she was letting some asshole play with her mind. Anger consumed her and she vowed no one was going to stop her now that she'd made up her mind.

Chapter Nine

Cain was working with one of the colts in the corral near the barn, and when he caught Cash storming toward him, he couldn't help watching the way her breasts jiggled beneath her T-shirt, or the way her hips and ass swayed as she walked. When she was closer and he got a glimpse of her face she looked mad. He wondered if the doctor had given her the all clear. Being careful not to spook the young horse he moved closer to the rail of corral.

"Cash, did doc give you the all clear?" he asked loud enough for her to hear but not frighten his current charge.

"Yes, sir," she snapped, giving him a glare. Then she saluted him.

If Cain had been alone he would have vaulted over the fence rail, slung her over his shoulder and carried her back to the house where he could pull her jeans down and spank her ass for her attitude. But he wasn't alone and several of the hands were looking at her as if she'd lost her mind. And she may well have since she was goading him. He wondered if she was doing it on purpose so she would end up between him and his brothers in the bedroom, but quickly rejected that idea. Cash wasn't like any other woman he'd ever met and he knew she wasn't into using feminine wiles to get what she wanted. She was too direct and honest. So what the hell was she all so fired up over?

Cain scanned the faces of the men watching Cash as she walked into the barn. None of them were looking at her in a sexual way. Bruce had told him and Danny about his theory on the sabotage to the tack equipment. Since it was the only hypothesis any of them could come up with, he and his brothers, as well as Harry and David, were going to be extra vigilant. David would have told Harry by now and he would be on alert as well. If someone was out to make trouble because they were trying to woo Cash, then he was going to be watching her intently. There was no way in hell he was letting her get hurt because of him and his brothers. He didn't want her getting caught in the crossfire.

With a sigh he turned back to the colt and started walking it in circles again. But no matter how hard he tried he couldn't get the image of Cash naked on the table from his head. Every time he managed it and his pants were more or less comfortable again, he saw her in his mind's eye and was hard an instant later. It was pure hell walking around with semi and permanent hard-on all the time.

"Cain." Cash's yell reached him a moment before she came racing out of the barn. He didn't even think about the horse. He was over that fence and had her in his arms moments later.

"What's wrong? Are you hurt?"

"No." She pushed against his chest. "Let me go, I'm fine."

"Then what's up?"

"The feed has been contaminated."

"What? Fuck!"

Cain released Cash, and she led him into the barn and the feed bins against the back wall where the lids were propped open. He looked into each bin and felt his anger rise. Someone had mixed corn into the food. Everyone knew that corn could give horses colic and cause a lot of problems.

"I'll get some garbage bags so we can trash it," Cash said and headed out after he gave her a nod.

Cain was so full of rage he wanted to hit something but he kept it contained so he wouldn't frighten Cash. He picked up a shovel and waited till she came back with a roll of trash bags. Between the two of them they had the food bins cleaned out and bags set aside to be disposed of later.

"I'm going to head into town for some more feed." Cain set the shovel aside. "Can you let Brutus and Danny know where I've gone?"

"Sure."

Cain didn't like the incidents happening around the ranch but until they caught someone in the act there was nothing he could do about it. He hated that one of the hands had it in for them but at least they had directed their anger at them and not Cash. If that had been the case he wouldn't ever let her out of his sight. He and his brothers had plans to finish what they started this morning, tonight, and there wasn't any way they were letting her keep them away. She was the love of his life, but now they had to get her to take a chance on them. He would do anything to be able to hold her in his arms for the rest of his life but first they had to get through that protective shell she had around her heart, and he wasn't giving up until she was theirs.

* * * *

Cash watched Cain stride angrily from the barn. She was just as pissed off as he was that someone had tried to make the horses sick. They were in her care and if they had gotten ill she would have been responsible. Was someone trying to get her fired? Anger consumed her and she looked about the barn. There was no incriminating evidence left and she doubted any one had seen whoever had tried to sabotage her job. The hair on her nape prickled and she spun toward the tack room. She couldn't see anyone about but she couldn't shake the sensation of being watched. Deciding to leave was her only option so she did just that. As soon as she was out in the sunshine she felt a whole lot better.

Bruce was just coming from the house so she walked over to meet him. He eyed her body up and down until she was standing only a few feet away. Cash told Bruce what she had discovered and watched as his face turned to cold hard granite and he ground his teeth together.

"Show me," he demanded.

She led him to the barn and opened one of the garbage bags of now-useless feed.

"Did you see anyone about?"

"No, the barn was empty when I came in."

"There is something going on here and I don't like it. You are going to be staying with us until we can clear this up."

"Look, I…"

"No." Bruce moved closer, gripped her waist, and lifted her up until their eyes were level. The move turned her on to no end. The show of strength got her juices flowing even more. "Someone obviously has it in for me and my brothers. I don't want you getting caught up in the line of fire. You're just an itty bit of a woman and I couldn't live with myself if you got hurt because of me, us. I know you're independent but please humor me on this."

Cash felt guilty because she knew this had nothing to with them and everything to do with her. She wanted to argue and refuse his and his brothers' protection but from the implacable look in his eyes he wasn't about to back down. But if she told them about what she found in her room she could see all of them trying to keep her under lock and key. And that she didn't want. As much as she appreciated their concern she had been taking care of herself for a long time, so why should now be any different? Besides if they knew about the flower and the note she could be putting them in harm's way.

"Dinner's at seven," Bruce said as he lowered her feet back to the ground. "Make sure you are there or I'll come looking for you."

Cash turned away and began to clean the water troughs, muttering to herself about overbearing men. Bruce was scouting the barn but after about five minutes left with a frustrated sigh.

Cain came back with the food and emptied the bags into the feed bins with Danny's help. She watched their muscles bulging and rippling as they carried the heavy bags and cursed her body's response. By the time she worked up the courage to get what she wanted from them she would be one big puddle of goo.

Dinner time came around all too fast. She had hurried back to her cabin and after making sure no one had been inside she showered and changed and headed up to the house. She still had a few jeans and shirts in the spare room of the ranch house but had opted for some privacy and trying to get her raucous nerves under control. Her stomach was a fluttering mess and she had no idea how the hell she was supposed to eat when it wouldn't settle down. Giving a mental shrug she pushed her shoulders back and headed to the main house.

* * * *

He watched her as she walked toward the boss's place. He'd hoped his little messages would have gotten through to her but she was either too stupid to get it or just plain blasé. If one of those assholes touched her one more time he might just snap. Didn't they get that she was his? He couldn't take much more of this shit. His wife had to learn her place and he was just the man to do it. It looked like he was going to have to up the ante. Maybe then she would realize he wasn't going to put up with her being such a slut.

He hurried back to his cabin and shut the door. None of his workmates knew about his collection and that was the way he wanted to keep it. Everywhere he looked was his beautiful bride. Her face glowed with the love she felt for him with her dressed in her wedding finery. His walls were covered with her pictures and when he looked at them he remembered each time he had taken the photo. She was so beautiful she should have been an angel. He loved the pictures of her in various states of undress as well as the nudes, but the bridal shots were his favorite. When he saw them he could see her declaring her love for him over and over again.

He knelt down and pulled the box from beneath his bed. The stack of photo albums was hidden beneath the blanket his mother had knitted for him years before. After lovingly putting the blanket aside he removed the albums from the box, sat down on the side of the bed and started turning the pages. Every time he looked at the pictures he knew that Cash was meant to be his. He'd taken a lot of pictures of her over the last six months and would soon need to buy another photo album. His walls were covered with her image and all his books were full. Yes, he needed to get new albums soon.

She was such a pure, intelligent, pretty, hard-working woman and every time he looked at her image his heart clenched and his dick got hard. He'd been careful to keep his love hidden from the other hands, but now that those bastards were here and a danger to him and his wife they had to be stopped.

He stroked a finger down her beautiful face and over her hair. This photo had been taken nearly two months ago. She had been sitting in the shade of a tree reading a book, totally oblivious to everything and everyone around her. Turning the page, his breath caught in his throat when he saw her petite, sexy, curvy body with small wisps of silk and lace covering her in strategic places. This picture had been taken only four weeks ago. He remembered that night well. He had stood outside her bedroom window for a long time hoping and waiting. His patience had eventually paid off and he was able to get the perfect photo when the curtains to her window had moved aside in the breeze. The only thing that would have been better was if she had been naked. There weren't near enough photos of her in her purest form and he wanted more. Maybe he would have the opportunity to get another photo of her soon.

He quickly vetoed that idea. The optimum situation would be to get Cashmere Woodall in his arms and have her in his cabin to do with as he wished.

Yes, my boy. That is what you need to do. That girl is meant to be yours. Don't let anyone take her away from you.

He smiled when he heard his momma's voice in his head. She'd said she would never leave him and she hadn't, not even the day she had died. He spent the next hour looking at the image of his perfect wife. He couldn't take the ache in his cock anymore so he undid his belt, opened his jeans and stroked his hard flesh as he imagined what he would do to Cashmere once she was his. Moments later his seed spewed from his dick and over the plastic-coated photos. With a smile he wiped his up his cum with his momma's blanket and carefully packed everything away. He laid down on his bed and knew without a doubt that she would be his forevermore once he was able to get to her. It had to be soon. His momma's voice echoed his sentiments in his head.

* * * *

Dinner was full of tension, and even though Cash kept her head down and her mouth shut, she felt their eyes on her. They hadn't taken their gazes off her since she sat down, and her body was so fraught with strain she thought she just might snap. She'd only eaten half the steak and a few mouthfuls of salad but she couldn't eat another bite, so instead she pushed the food around her plate, making it look like she had been eating.

"I've had enough of this shit." Cain pushed his chair back from the table and stood. He stalked around the wooden furniture, his eyes pinned to hers and she thought she may have had an inkling for how prey felt when being stalked by a predator. He didn't stop until he was standing right before her. He held his hand out to her and waited.

Cash nibbled on her lip as she tried to decide what to do and then she heard Harry's words in her head. *Are you willing to throw away something that could be special because you're afraid of getting hurt?*

Taking a deep breath and hoping she wasn't making the biggest mistake of her life, she placed her hand in his. Everyone in the room knew the significance of her action and some of the tension in the air alleviated.

Cain didn't say anything but the tightness in his face waned and then he helped her to her feet. Keeping hold of her hand, he led her out of the kitchen through the living room and down the hall. She didn't have to look back over her shoulder to see if Bruce and Danny were following, because she could feel their eyes on her ass. Cain flicked the light on in the room she'd stayed in for the last week and released her hand to close the blinds. When he was done he turned around to face her.

"Get out of those clothes, baby."

Although she'd been naked in front of them once before, she felt a little shy and vulnerable with an audience and instead of pulling her shirt over her head she played with the hem of it. She jumped when large, warm hands landed on her shoulder.

"Easy, sweet cheeks." Bruce's warm, moist breath caressed her neck just before he kissed the sensitive spot under her ear. "There's nothing to be afraid of. We'll take things nice and slow."

"Let me help you, baby." Cain walked closer and then reached for the hem of her shirt. He didn't try to pull it off but stood there watching her. His hazel eyes were so full of hunger she couldn't help but react. Her breathing grew shallow, her nipples pebbled and her pussy clenched. When she let go of the material he pulled the shirt up over her head. His quiet groan let her know that he definitely liked what he saw. Since she'd only removed her underwear from the washer before coming to dinner, she'd gone without a bra.

"So goddamn sexy," Cain said in a raspy voice. "You have the most perfect tits I've ever seen in my life. Hold them up for me, Brutus."

Cash couldn't help but whimper when Bruce's long, thick callused fingers smoothed over her flesh as he moved his arms around her shoulders and body to cup them. He lifted them up and held them high in an offering. Cain leaned down and forward and swiped each tip with his tongue. Cash gasped as pleasure washed over her and zinged down to her cunt. Her head bumped back onto Bruce's chest and she closed her eyes.

"Open your eyes, sugar," Danny demanded. "We want to see your pleasure."

Her eyelids lifted and she saw Danny standing next to Cain. He gave his twin brother a slight shove until they were standing side by side in front of her. And then they both leaned down and took a nipple into their mouths. Cash moaned and arched her back, pushing her breasts forward for firmer contact. They took her hint and started sucking them harder.

Bruce's hands caressed down her sides and then over her waist and hips and across her stomach. His fingers worked on the button of her jeans and then her zipper was being lowered, and then he pushed her jeans and panties down over her hips, then down her legs. She could feel his moist breath puffing against the cheeks of her ass and then he tapped one leg.

"Step out, Cash."

She lifted a leg, and when she wobbled he placed his hand on her ass to steady her as he pulled her jeans and panties off over her ankle and foot. Then he repeated the process on her other leg. When she didn't feel him move behind her she became curious and was about to turn her head to look over her shoulder, but his hand moved from the center of her ass and then he was gripping both cheeks in both of his hands. She groaned when he kneaded her fleshy globes and then cried out when he removed one hand and slipped a finger between her legs to her pussy hole.

"Spread your legs for me, sweet cheeks."

Cash shifted her feet apart and held her breath when she felt Bruce exhale right over her slit. Danny released her nipple with a pop and then stood upright. He cupped her face and stared deeply into her eyes, and then he bent down and kissed her. Just as his lips connected with hers, Bruce swiped his tongue along her wet folds. The keen she let loose got lost in Danny's mouth as he devoured her.

Her whole body was shaking with desire and she didn't know how much longer she would be able to stand. With Cain suckling at her breast, Danny kissing her wildly, hungrily, and Bruce licking her pussy, she was overwhelmed with sensations. It was hard not to cry out when Bruce's mouth left her aching cunt, but then both Cain and Danny lifted their heads and stepped back. Bruce's hard, muscled chest brushed against her back and it was only then she realized that he had removed his shirt. The warmth from his body caused her to shiver.

"Let's get you comfortable, sweet cheeks." That was the only warning she got before she was swept from her feet up into Bruce's arms and carried over to the bed. He placed her in the centre of the mattress and then climbed on with her at her feet. Gently prying her legs apart his big callused hands smoothed up and down her upper thighs, gradually working their way to her inner leg. The bed dipped on either side of her and when she looked at Cain and Danny she saw that they were naked.

She perused their bodies with her eyes, first one, then the other. They were so similar in looks but each had very different personalities and she had no trouble telling them apart. Danny sat on his haunches while she studied him, totally comfortable in his own skin, and she ate him up with her gaze. His shoulders were wide and his pecs looked rock hard. When he moved, they rippled. The muscles in his abs were ripped and she could see each rigid line of delineation between them. The tip of his cock was a deep purple color and the broad mushroom-shaped tip was near his belly button. He was thick and hard and his cock pulsed with each beat of his heart. His balls hung heavy between his spread thighs and she wanted to reach out and touch them to see if they felt as soft as they looked.

Movement from her other side drew her attention and she looked into Cain's hunger-filled eyes. He was nearly the spitting image of his brother but so very much an individual. His shoulders were as broad as Danny's and he was just as cut. His cock wasn't as wide as Danny's but it looked like it was longer. The tip of his penis was an angry-looking red color and she could see a clear drop of liquid in the slit of the bulbous head.

Bruce's hands slid up her inner thighs, pushing her legs farther apart. When she glanced down toward him she saw that he was naked, too. He must have removed his clothes while she was ogling his brothers. Cash had never seen a more muscular man than him. He was built to perfection. His shoulders looked hard and each time he moved his hands on her legs his pecs shifted. Bruce's chest was thick and then it tapered down to his torso and abs. The man didn't have a six pack. He was so ripped that each and every muscle in his stomach and lower belly showed beneath his skin. The tip of his erection was above his navel and when she let her eyes travel down his length she got a bit nervous. He was so damn big he looked thicker than her wrist.

Cash licked her lips nervously and tried to close her legs but Bruce's grip on her thighs firmed and stopped her.

"I know I'm a big man, sweet cheeks, but trust me. I won't do anything to hurt you, Cash. I'll go nice and slow with you, baby."

Cash licked her lips but couldn't take her eyes off his huge cock. Cain reached out and gripped her chin and then turned her head toward him. He was lying on his side, resting his head on his other hand, but as their gazes connected he lowered his head. His tongue pushed his way between her lips and teeth and then he glided it along hers. Hands kneaded her breasts and then thumbs strummed over her turgid, sensitive peaks and she moaned with pleasure.

The bed dipped between her thighs and then she cried out when Bruce licked her from clit to ass and back again. The fire which had begun to diminish began to burn hotter and she couldn't stay still.

Bruce splayed one hand over her belly and pubis and applied pressure, trying to hold her still, but that only seemed to compound the bliss building inside her. A thick finger rimmed her pussy hole while Bruce's tongue lapped over her clit. Her legs were shaking and taut with tension but also felt weak. She moaned when he pushed a finger up inside her and then winced slightly at the pinch.

Cain released her mouth and held her face between his big hands. "Just relax for Bruce, baby. He's going to give you an orgasm while he takes your virginity."

How do they know I'm a virgin?

Cash must have shown shock or a similar expression on her face because Cain smiled down into her eyes. "Yes, Cash we know you've never been with a man before. Do you know how fucking special you are? You won't ever be with anyone else but me and my brothers. You're ours now, baby."

Cash closed her eyes and moaned as Bruce pumped a thick finger in and out of her pussy while laving her clit. He hadn't once stopped his tongue from caressing over the sensitive bundle of nerves and she could feel her juices flowing from her sheath. Each time he pressed his fingers forward he gained a little more depth and the friction inside her was building to mammoth proportions. Her head moved restlessly on the pillow but she couldn't move far with Cain still holding her face.

"Open your eyes, sugar," Danny demanded after releasing her nipple from his mouth. She found herself obeying him immediately. "Keep them open and on Cain, Cash."

Cash whimpered and although her eyes wanted to close she kept them open. The fire was so hot inside her now she didn't know how much more she could take. Her vision grew hazy but she kept her lids up. Her belly jumped and her legs shook. She couldn't have moved if she wanted to, but she didn't want to. Liquid warmth formed in her womb, making it feel achy and heavy, but the warmth spread out until it was consuming her. The muscles inside were so rigid and the pleasure so great she strained toward it. Fingers squeezed her nipples hard and she screamed as the coil inside her snapped. Wave upon wave of rapture washed over her and she cried out again when Bruce thrust his finger into her as far as it would go. She felt a slight pinch and then she was flying up to the stars again. Her body shook and quavered as nirvana swept over her.

When she came back into her body, she smiled and sighed with satiation. Three sets of hands were running over her, lightly calming her back down from her climactic high. She'd never felt so sexy or sated in her life and she knew there was more to come. She couldn't wait to have them inside her.

Chapter Ten

Bruce was so goddamned turned on he was shaking. He couldn't wait to get inside that slick wet pussy. Now that he'd taken care of Cash's virgin barrier and knew he wouldn't hurt her he couldn't hold back. He sat up between her legs and moved in closer. Cash looked like a sex goddess with her cheeks all flushed and rosy and that satisfied smile on her face.

Danny nudged him on the arm and passed him a condom. He brought the packet up to his mouth and used his teeth to rip it open and then donned the latex sheath. Gripping her hips he leaned forward and kissed her lightly on the lips. She moaned and then licked across his mouth. He wondered if she liked the taste of her own cum, but that thought flitted away when she slid her tongue into his mouth. They kissed wildly and passionately and then he lifted up.

"Are you ready for me, sweet cheeks?" Bruce slipped his hands beneath her ass and squeezed. She nodded and licked her lips again.

"Tell me if I hurt you, Cash. The last thing I want to do is cause you pain."

She nodded once more and then Bruce lined his cock up with her pussy and began to push in. She was so damn tight and he didn't want to force himself inside her, so he kept a tight rein on himself. Sweat beaded on his brow and began to run down the side of his face. Even with her being so wet he was having trouble getting the broad head of his cock to go inside her.

Cain and Danny were both watching and keeping an eye on Cash. When Cain rolled off the bed and left the room he wondered where his brother was going. His question was answered moments later when he came back with a tube of lube. Bruce sighed gratefully, took the bottle from his brother and pulled his cock back from Cash's cunt. He squirted a liberal amount of personal gel onto his condom-covered cock and then wiped his hand on the towel Danny proffered.

Bruce slid his hands under Cash's knees and lifted until her ass and hips left the bed. He spread her wide and then glided his cock through her folds. Aligning the crown of his dick with her hole once more, he pressed forward. This time he watched as his penis separated her flesh and finally popped through her tight tissue. He glanced up to her face to make sure he wasn't hurting her, but Danny was kissing her and Cain was sucking on one of her nipples.

"Are you okay, sweet cheeks?"

Cash moaned and pushed her hips up in silent demand. Bruce groaned with relief and slowly began to push inside her. Her pussy was so fucking tight and wet but as he pressed his way inside her, he knew he had found heaven on Earth. She was home and he would do anything to keep her by his side. Taking his time was one of the hardest things he'd ever had to do, especially when he wanted to surge inside her till his balls connected with her ass and then slam into her again and again. He rocked his hips slowly, advancing and retreating, giving her body time to adjust to his penetration and width. By the time he was all the way inside her, he was covered in a light sheen of sweat.

Danny released her mouth and then latched onto her free nipple. Cain and Danny suckled at her breasts as Bruce began to love his woman in earnest. With each pump of his hips he increased the speed and depth of his penetration until his pelvis was slapping against her ass. Cash moaned and gasped with pleasure as he shuttled his cock in and out of her cunt.

"So good," Cash groaned. "I can feel it coming."

"Yes, sweet cheeks. That's it. Give yourself to me. Let go, Cash. I want to feel you come on my cock."

Bruce was on edge. The tingling warmth in his lower back warned of his impending orgasm but he wasn't about to go over before Cash. He glanced toward Cain and gave him a nod and then watched his brother's hand caress down Cash's belly to the top of her slit.

Cain made little circles on her clit, getting faster and faster as Bruce pounded her harder. Her pussy muscles rippled around his cock and she covered him with her cream. She was on the edge and so was he. He shifted slightly, which changed the angle of his thrusting cock, and he knew he'd found her sweet spot when she gasped. He shoved into her again and again and just as he thought he was going first, Cash's cunt clamped down hard on his penis and she screamed. Bruce shuttled into her one, two, three more times and then he froze. He shouted as the tingling warmth spread around to his groin, his balls drew up, and then he quivered as he shot load after load of cum into the condom. The orgasm seemed to last forever, one of the most powerful and lengthy climaxes he had ever experienced, but it was over too soon. His legs were shaking and he was gasping for breath.

Cain and Danny moved aside when he released her legs and came down on top of her. He buried his face against her neck and wrapped his arms around her body, but kept his weight on his elbows.

"Never, sweet cheeks. I've never felt anything like that before. You're amazing." Bruce lifted up and kissed her reverently on the lips. *God, she's beautiful.* Her eyes were still glazed from her climax and her cheeks were flushed. His heart filled with joy and hope. Now that she'd let him make love to her, would she let him and his brothers into her life permanently? He wanted to ask her but knew it wasn't the right time. He'd just have to be patient and hope that she felt the same way for them.

* * * *

Cash had thought the previous orgasms they had given her were big, but they paled in comparison to what she had just experienced.

Having a cock moving inside her was the most beautiful, poignant experience of her life and she wanted more. She should have been feeling satiated and tired from such a big climax, and even though she was replete, just looking at Danny and Cain got her libido revving again. Cash wanted them to make love to her, too.

"How are you feeling, baby?" Cain brushed her hair away from her face.

"Good."

"Are you sore, sugar?" Danny splayed a hand on her belly.

"No. I want to make love with you both, too."

"Are you sure, Cash? We don't want to make you sore." Cain leaned down and kissed her forehead.

Cash fell a little more for them because even though Danny and Cain were horny, they weren't pushing themselves on her, but she wanted them just as much as they wanted her. She rolled over onto her stomach and then pushed up to her hands and knees. Danny was closest so she reached out and wrapped her hand around his cock and pumped it up and down a few times.

"Fuck," Danny groaned. "That feels so good, sugar."

It's about to get better, Cash thought to herself. She leaned forward and swirled her tongue all around the head of his cock. When he moaned as her tongue swiped over a spot under the head of his dick, she did it again and then again. Danny threaded his fingers into her hair and gripped it. "Suck me, sugar. Please?"

Cash opened her mouth and sucked his cock in as far as she could take him without gagging. The grip on her hair got tighter and he moaned again. "Fuck yeah, Cash, just like that." She got into a rhythm of advance and retreat, suctioning on his cock as she drew back and then laving beneath the head before sucking him back in.

Cash jumped slightly when warm hands landed on her hips but she didn't stop sucking on Danny's cock. Cain shoved a leg in between hers and gave her a slight nudge so she parted them further. Bruce came back from the bathroom and watched her avidly as she gave Danny head. He reached out and rolled one of her nipples between thumb and finger.

Cain skimmed his fingers through her wet folds and then gently dipped inside.

"You're so fucking wet, baby. You like sucking Danny's cock, don't you?"

"Hmm," Cash hummed her agreement.

"Oh fuck. Hurry the hell up Cain, she's too good at this, I'm not gonna last."

Cain's front covered her back and he moved his hips, which skimmed his cock along her slit. When she was about to pull off Danny and beg him to take her, she felt the tip at her entrance. And then he was pushing into her. She moaned around Danny's cock and he moaned with her. As Cain pressed inside she felt her sensitive tissue stretch and relished the slight pleasurable burn. He was so big from this angle, but so damn good.

Cain rocked his hips, gaining speed and depth with every pass. By the time he was all the way inside her, Cash felt like she was on the verge of orgasm again. Leaning on one hand she reached out and cupped Danny's balls. The skin was velvet soft but his testicles felt hard. She gently rolled them in their sac and sucked his cock down deep.

"Jesus, sugar, so fucking good," Danny gasped. "I'm gonna come, sweetie, let go."

Cash held his testes firmly but not enough to hurt him, breathed deeply through her nose, and swallowed around the head of his cock. Danny's penis seemed to expand in her mouth and then it jerked as cum shot out the tip, across her tongue and down her throat. She swallowed convulsively, not wanting to lose any of his essence and didn't let up until he pulled from her mouth and then he slumped onto the bed beside her.

A slap landed on her ass and she turned to look over her shoulder. "That's for not minding Danny. We control what happens in the bedroom, baby, not you."

Oh yeah! We'll just see about that.

Cash placed her hands firmly on the bed, spread her legs wider and pushed back against Cain. He growled low in his throat and slapped her ass again, and as he shoved forward she pushed back. Their lovemaking had become a playful power struggle and she wasn't about to let him win. Their flesh slapped together, the sound echoing in the room as they fought for supremacy. But he was much stronger and more experienced than her so she should have known he would win. He leaned over her body and swept her arms out from under her. Her shoulders hit the bed and her arms were lying on the mattress above her head. Cain shifted until his whole body was blanketing hers and he held her hands down.

His hips began to piston fast and hard, shuttling his cock in and out of her pussy rapidly. His breath caressed her ear when he spoke in a deep gravelly voice. "I'm close, help her over."

Bruce moved closer and then she felt his fingers on her pussy, at the top of her slit and she knew there was no way she would be able to hold off her impending climax. But that didn't mean she couldn't take Cain with her, so she squeezed her internal muscles as hard as she could.

"Oh fuck!" Cain roared.

Bruce squeezed her clit and Cash was lost. The bliss which had been building erupted into great surges of rapture. She shook and quivered as nirvana assailed her. It rolled over her in great waves as Cain rode her through the euphoria. Cash was only vaguely aware of Cain's shout but she felt each jerk and pulse of his cock as he too reached his peak. Never in her life had she imagined such rhapsody and such an emotional connection. The casing surrounding her heart shattered and the emptiness inside filled with love and elation. She wanted to shout from the rooftops but she hadn't heard those words from her men, and she wasn't about to say them until they did. Until she knew for certain that they really cared for her she was going to keep her emotions close to her chest. She knew what it felt like to be rejected and wasn't about to put herself up for a fall. Although they had told her she was theirs and that they cared for her, that wasn't love.

Hands smoothed up and down her arms and Cain kissed her neck and shoulder, then gently withdrew from her body. Cash collapsed on the bed and closed her eyes. She hoped by keeping her eyes closed they couldn't see how she felt and tried to build that wall back up around her heart. But now that it was shattered she couldn't do it.

"What's wrong, Cash?" Bruce shifted closer, wrapped his arms around her, pulled her to her side and then into the curve of his body until he was spooning her.

"Nothing." She sighed and pushed her ass into his groin. The bed dipped in front of her and she knew Danny had scooted closer and then a hand landed on her shin and she realized that Cain was back from the bathroom.

"Open your eyes, sugar," Danny demanded, and she found herself obeying. "What's going through that pretty little head of yours?"

"Not much," Cash hedged.

"Look at me, baby," Cain ordered.

Cash lifted her head and met his eyes. When she did her heart stuttered and her belly fluttered. "Do you think we don't care for you, Cashmere? Did you think that was all just lust?"

"Cash, don't you realize that we gave you orders about not working because we couldn't stand to see you in pain and pushing yourself when it wasn't necessary?" Bruce asked.

Danny and Bruce maneuvered Cash onto her back where they could all see her and she could see them without having to turn too far. She wanted to ask them why they wanted her but bit her lip with uncertainty instead.

"Do you think we go around fucking virgins just for the hell of it?" Cain snapped angrily. "Do you think so little of us?"

"No," Cash answered honestly, sighing. She could see that they cared for her, but it was the extent of that caring she was uncertain of.

Bruce got up onto his knees and then helped her to sit up so that her back was up against the headboard with a pillow behind her. He took her face between his hands and stared deeply into her eyes.

"I love you, sweet cheeks. Why are you so afraid of that?"

Tears pricked her eyes and then flowed down her cheeks. Elation swept over her that this big, strong, muscular man wasn't scared to tell her how he felt.

"I'm not afraid, just cautious. Don't you understand why, after hearing about what my father did to me?"

Bruce sighed and let her face go. Cain tapped her leg, garnering her attention. "Do you think that we'd hurt you? Haven't you realized yet that we would do *anything* to protect you?"

"We know you have feelings for us, sugar," Danny said. "We love you. God, we've never said that to another woman before."

Cash sobbed and covered her mouth. The words were on the tip of her tongue but she couldn't say them. Couldn't, wouldn't put herself out there to be hurt again.

"I love you, baby," Cain declared. "We want to spend the rest of our lives with you. We're planning on moving our ranch to Slick Rock so you can move in with us. Don't you want to be with us?"

Cash scrambled over Danny and off the bed. She gathered up her clothes and headed for the door. When she looked back over her shoulder pain pierced her heart at the dejected, apathetic expressions on their faces, but she just couldn't.

"I'm sorry. I can't," Cash cried and hurried from the room. She stopped in the living room and dressed quickly before heading out to her cabin. Tears streamed from her eyes making her vision blurry and she was in so much pain she wanted to double over. She'd wanted to tell them that she loved them, had nearly done so several times but then she thought of how even her own father couldn't love her and had come to the conclusion that she was unlovable. She just wasn't cut out to be in a relationship. There had to be something wrong with her. Why couldn't she accept that what they'd said was true?

Cash closed the door to her cabin behind her and slid down to the floor. Her body still hummed with satiated desire from their love making and she thought back over the weeks and how each of them had looked out for her. The despondency and fear which had invaded her heart dissipated and in its place exultation reined.

It was only as she sat there on the floor with her arms around her legs and her head on her knees that she realized what they said was heartfelt and not lust driven. Why would they tell her they loved her after they'd taken her body? If they were feeding her a line wouldn't they have said so beforehand if they were just trying to get into her pants?

Cash groaned. She was so fucked up and stupid. She had just rejected the loves of her life out of fear and didn't know how to fix it. Her body was aching in a good way because of their recent loving but also because she was apart from her men. She had to fix what she'd done and there was only one way she knew how.

Firming her resolve to get back her men, she rose to her feet and headed for the bathroom. She was going to clean up and put on her new red dress and shoes and she was going to go and get what she wanted. Bruce, Cain and Danny were hers and she wanted to spend the rest of her life by their sides, loving them and growing old with them.

After showering she dried off, wrapped a towel around her and walked into her bedroom, aiming for the closet where her lone dress hung. Just as she opened the door to the robe pain exploded in her skull. She cried out and reached for the wardrobe door, but her vision was already blurry and she missed and went tumbling to the floor onto her side.

She saw work boots close to her face and as she followed the legs up with her eyes another hit landed on her head and she knew no more.

Chapter Eleven

Rage permeated his soul as he stood in the shadows and watched their silhouettes against the blinds. There was no way he was letting her get away from him, not when he'd spent the last few months planning. She was a slut just like his mother and every other woman alive. He was going to have to punish her and excise the demons inside her out of her.

She was supposed to be his. He'd known she had been pure but not anymore. She didn't deserve to be his wife now, she was just like his momma had been, spreading her legs for anything in pants. He'd looked forward to initiating her to love but not now, not when she'd sullied her body by letting them touch her, fuck her.

He'd seen the tears on her face as she'd hurried back to her cabin and hadn't had an ounce of sympathy for her. She'd known she was his and yet she'd still let them have that pure body. He'd warned her and now she was going to have to pay. Being careful to stay in the shadows, he kept his step light and followed her back home. He crept up onto the porch and listened as she cried near the door. After a bit she moved away and he heard her walking toward her bedroom. Glancing around to make sure no one was watching, he turned the door knob and slipped inside. He could hear the shower running and he went into the kitchen, looking for a weapon. Sitting on the bench top was a heavy stone mortar and pestle. He snickered as he picked up the heavy bowl. Tiptoeing into her bedroom he stood leaning against the wall and waited patiently. It wasn't long before she came out wrapped in a towel, and she didn't even notice that he was there. She walked toward her closet and opened the door.

With her back turned to him it was easy to get closer, and he raised his arm and brought the stone down hard on the side of her head. He laughed when she cried out with pain and tried to catch the door, falling to the floor instead. She tried to look up at him through heavy eyelids but before she could he brought the stone mortar down on her head again and watched as her eyes closed.

* * * *

Cain grabbed his clothes and pulled them on. His chest ached and he wanted to rub the pain away, but he knew that wouldn't help. He'd been so sure that Cashmere loved them as much as they loved her and a couple of times he could have sworn that she was about to tell them how she felt but as she opened her mouth she stopped and clamped her lips shut again.

"What the hell are we supposed to do now?" Danny asked with a sigh. Cain had been wondering the same thing, but he didn't have a clue. He and his brothers had opened up with Cash and even though she hadn't rejected their love she hadn't been brave enough to reciprocate. It wasn't that she didn't love them, he had seen it in her eyes. She just hadn't had the courage to tell them how she felt.

Cain headed to the kitchen and snagged three beers from the fridge. After handing the other two to his now-dressed brothers when they entered the room, he twisted the top off his own bottle and took a long swig. He stared out the window and gazed toward Cash's cabin. Lights twinkled around the edges of the curtained windows and he wondered what she was doing. He'd seen the tears in her eyes when she'd left. Was she sitting on the small couch crying her eyes out?

"We need to go and talk to her," Brutus said finally breaking the silence. "We have to convince her that we really love her."

"We already tried, Brutus," Cain mumbled. "I don't want to put myself up for another slap down."

"Cash didn't do that." Danny took a slug from his bottle. "Not once did she say that we were lying or that she didn't believe us. All she said was 'I can't.'"

"You're right," Cain agreed and put his now-empty bottle on the counter and turned to face his brothers. "She didn't reject us, she's running scared again."

Bruce rose to his feet. "This has to stop now. I can't let her stay away from us. If we let her keep her distance we are gonna lose her and I'm not prepared to let that happen. Let's go and talk some sense into our woman."

"Do you think we should leave it for tonight and wait until tomorrow?" Danny suggested. "Let's give her time to calm down and then we can talk to her rationally. We'll all be calmer after a good night's sleep."

"Good idea," Cain agreed. "But first thing tomorrow we talk to her. I'm not giving up until she tells us she love us."

Cain glanced out the window once more and then headed toward his bedroom. He hoped that he would be able to sleep but with his mind in such turmoil and his gut so knotted up he didn't think he would be able to close his eyes for hours. But one thing was for certain, Cash wasn't going to be leaving his sights until he had her where he wanted her, in their bed and entrenched in her heart and soul.

* * * *

Cash's head was pounding so bad she felt sick to her stomach. She couldn't remember where she was or what had happened or why she was ill. She'd never been one to overindulge in alcohol often but thought that she may have a hangover, but she couldn't remember drinking the night before.

It wasn't just her head that was aching, her arms and legs were sore, too. Her wrist and ankles felt like she had a band around them and when she tried to move, she couldn't. Her hands and feet were numb and she was so cold she was shaking. Opening her eyes to slits caused pain to pierce her skull and nausea roil in her stomach. She slammed them shut and turned her head to the side, moaning when it hurt to move. The movement caused her to realize that she had something tied around her face and over her mouth. God, her brain was so fuzzy she wasn't functioning on all cylinders. She lay still, breathing evenly and deeply through her nose until the pain in her skull eased slightly, as did the nausea in her belly.

This time when she opened her eyes the pain wasn't as bad, but the light shining into the room was minimal since the curtains were closed. Glancing around the room she couldn't work out where she was. She'd never been here before. When she tried to sit up and couldn't she tilted her head back and saw the leather straps tied tightly around her wrists and to the metal slats of the bedhead. And then she lifted her head and looked down to her feet and realized her ankles were also tied up.

Cash began to shake with fear. She had no idea where she was or who had taken her but she was in deep shit. She wished that she'd shown one of her men that threatening letter and told them that she loved them. Now that her life was in danger and she may never see them again she realized she had been a complete and utter coward for not telling them how she felt. She may never get the chance to see their loving faces again and they would never know how much she cared for them. Tears leaked from her eyes and she cursed the fates and whoever had kidnapped her, but she wasn't going to let this asshole ruin her life when she found love for the first time. Taking as deep a breath as she could through her nose, she wiped her moist cheeks on both shoulders and began to work at getting the gag off. No matter how long it took or how hard it was, Cash was determined to escape.

* * * *

Danny knocked on Cash's front door again and waited for her to answer. He knew she was up because the lights were on, but she still hadn't come to the door. She was probably in the shower but he didn't want to wait to see her. Hoping he didn't piss her off by entering her place without an invitation he turned the door handle and cursed under his breath when he met no resistance. He was going to have to punish her for not locking her door, especially when she was living on a ranch with so many men. Her living room was neat and tidy as was her kitchen, so he headed to her bedroom.

Danny frowned when he realized her bathroom door was open with the light on and there was no sound of running water. Her closet door was open and her bed didn't look like it had been slept in.

"Cash, where are you?"

The hair on Danny's nape stood on end. Something wasn't right but he didn't know what. She wasn't here and he began to feel dread forming in the pit of his stomach. The only other place she could be was with Harry and David at their cabin, or in the bunkhouse. He spun on his heels and rushed toward Harry's. By the time he knocked on their door he was panting, but not from rushing. He was full of anxiety and he couldn't shake the pending doom which had lodged in his heart and wouldn't let go.

David answered the door but Danny didn't give him a chance to speak. "Is Cash here?"

"No, I thought she was with you and your brothers."

"She was but she got upset and left. Do you have any idea where she could be? She's not in her cabin and her bed hasn't been slept in."

"Shit. No I…"

"What's going on?" Harry asked as he came up behind David.

"I'm going back to search her cabin," Danny said before David could explain to Harry. "Can you let Brutus and Cain know where I am?"

"Of course," David replied, and Danny heard him begin explaining to Harry as he headed to the main house.

Danny went back to Cash's place and entered her bedroom. He glanced into the bathroom and saw the clothes she had been wearing the previous evening on the floor. As he walked over to her open closet he looked down and saw a dark stain on the carpet. He bent down and touched the spot and found it sticky. When he lifted his fingers and saw the reddish brown stain on his fingertips his heart stuttered. He brought his fingers to his nose and sniffed, but he already knew what he was seeing. The metallic scent of blood assailed his nostrils and he roared with pain. Someone had hurt and taken his woman.

Danny tried to get his emotions under control by breathing deeply and evenly a few times. When his anger and fear receded he looked about. It didn't look like a struggle had taken place so that meant that Cash had been taken unaware. He looked over to her closet and saw something grey on the floor. Being careful not to disturb any more evidence he skirted the blood and leaned over to see what it was. The heavy stone mortar bowl was lying on its side and had blood as well as a couple of strands of long dark hair stuck to it.

Just as he got to his feet and pulled his cell phone from his pocket Bruce and Cain entered the room. He quickly told them what he'd found and called 9-1-1. When he was patched through to the sheriff, Danny explained to Luke Sun-Walker what he'd found.

Luke told him not to touch anything and that he and Damon Osborne would be there as fast as possible.

Danny followed his brothers into the living room and he saw David and Harry standing in the doorway.

"Get all the hands together and saddled up," Danny barked out orders. "I want every inch of this ranch searched."

"Wait," Bruce said, "has anyone checked to see if Cash's car is still here?"

"I'm on it." Harry rushed away.

"We need to search in here," Cain said and headed toward the kitchen. "Whoever has her may have left a clue."

"Luke said not to touch anything," Danny explained.

"I won't," Cain replied, "but I have to do something. Our woman's hurt and needs us."

Danny nodded and headed back to the bedroom. He searched Cash's room and the bathroom and when he couldn't find anything else he sank down onto the side of her bed. Reaching for her pillow he brought it to his face and inhaled Cash's sweet scent. The thought of her out there hurt somewhere made him sick to his stomach. Tears pricked the back of his eyes but he didn't let them fall. His woman needed him to keep it together so he could help find her and when he did he wasn't letting her go ever again.

* * * *

Cash must have fallen asleep because when she opened her eyes the room was brighter than it had been before. Even though her head was pounding she didn't feel as sick, and for that she was thankful. With care, she slowly and carefully turned her head toward the window above the bed and saw a large tree not too far away. She frowned because that tree looked familiar. And then it hit her, it was familiar because it was on the ranch behind the bunkhouse and cabins. She was still on the ranch. One of the ranch hands must have hit her on the head and carried her from her home, but whom? No one had ever looked at her as if they were interested in her in a sexual way besides her three men. The only person who had approached her was Arty.

Could he have been the one to hurt her? She couldn't see him doing that. He was such a quiet man and didn't go out carousing on the weekend with the other hands, but he did ask her out not long ago and when she had refused she'd thought she'd seen anger on his face. If he was hiding his true personality then no one would even think to question him about her whereabouts. It looked like it was up to her to get out of this predicament. Hopefully he would be out working on the ranch, which would give her the time she needed to try and escape.

Cash brushed her face against her shoulder trying to pry the gag out of her mouth, but it was tied too tightly. She tugged on her hands but the leather around her wrists chafed and cut into her skin. Her shoulders were screaming with pain from being tied up for so long and her hands were numb, but she wasn't going to give up. There had to be some way she could get free or alert someone she was here. She pulled and tugged as hard as she could, but no matter how hard she tried the leather didn't budge. When she stopped to rest she was struggling to fill her lungs with oxygen because of the gag and she was exhausted. Her head was pounding and her hair was wet. There must be a cut on her head because it was stinging like a bitch and she may have made it bleed again with all her moving.

Her eyes drooped and no matter how hard she tried to keep them open she couldn't. With one last desperate jerk on her hands and legs she finally drifted into sleep.

* * * *

"I found something," Cain yelled just as he heard the sheriffs pull up.

Bruce rushed into the kitchen and noted Cain's pale face. His brother's gaze was fixed on the kitchen drawer open before him. He moved closer and blanched when he read the note. Cain reached out to pick it up but Bruce grabbed his wrist to stop him.

"Don't, it could have prints on it. Luke, get in here."

Luke walked over next to him and looked down. "Shit. When did she get this?"

"I don't know. If it was before today Cash never said a word."

"Did either of you touch it?"

"No," Bruce and Cain answered simultaneously.

"Good," Luke replied. "Damon, bring your kit in here."

Bruce and Cain moved out of the way and watched as Damon picked the note up with tweezers. He placed it on the counter and then began dusting it with powder. Only one set of prints showed up and Bruce hoped they weren't Cash's. Damon took out his phone and snapped a picture of the prints then sent it with a text message to forensics. He turned to face him and Cain.

"If those prints are on the system we should have a result within the hour. I also dusted that heavy bowl and if I had to hazard a guess the prints on there match these ones."

Harry and David came in and Bruce looked at them. "Any sign of her?"

"No." Harry frowned. "I don't get it. There should be some sort of tracks leading from the ranch but I can't find anything. No tire or horse tracks, just…nothing."

"What if she's still here?" Danny said, drawing their eyes. "What if someone on this ranch has her hidden away somewhere?"

"Search the barn," Bruce ordered, "including the hayloft, the feed bins, tack room, and all the stalls."

"Hang on," David said, and then turned to Harry. "Didn't Cash tell you that Arty had asked her out on a date?"

"Fuck, I forgot all about that, and yeah, he did. Cash said him approaching her was a surprise because she didn't think any of the hands looked at her like she was a woman."

"Where is Arty now?" Luke asked.

"He's out searching with the men," Harry answered.

"Does he live in one of the cabins or the bunkhouse?" Bruce moved toward the front door.

"A cabin," David replied as he followed Bruce outside.

The rest of the men followed and before long they were standing outside the cabin, which was the last one in the back of the bunkhouse. Bruce turned the handle and cursed when he found it locked. He glanced over his shoulder at his brothers and then moved back and kicked the door near the lock. The door burst open and bounced against the wall with a loud bang. He caught it with his hand before it swung back and hit him in the face.

Cash was lying on the bed, tethered up by wrists and ankles with the damaged tack. Her eyes were closed and she was wrapped up in a towel, which only just covered her modesty. Bruce hurried over to her and checked her pulse, his knees nearly buckling with relief when he felt the strong beat of her heart and her chest rose and fell as she breathed.

The wall of the cabin was covered with pictures of Cash. Her face had been cut out and put on magazine cut outs of women in wedding gowns. There were also photos of her as she sat on the sofa in her cabin and some of her nude as she came from her bathroom, and also in various states of undress. Rage consumed Bruce and even though he wanted to go and find Arty and beat the crap out of the sick bastard, his woman needed him more.

"Go and arrest his ass, Luke," Bruce commanded in a hoarse voice.

"You got it," Luke replied and he left with Damon, as well as Harry and David, on his heels.

"I've called the paramedics," Damon yelled out and Bruce nodded to let him know he'd heard him.

* * * *

Cain was so filled with rage he was shaking. Now that Cash had Brutus to take care of her he lit out of the cabin and followed Luke and Damon. When he heard footsteps beside him he looked up to see Danny was with him step for step.

Cain caught up with the two sheriffs, Harry, and David in the barn, and without a word he and his brother saddled and then mounted up. He kicked his mount into a gallop and heard the thundering hooves of the horse Danny was seated on a half stride behind him. He could hear yelling from Luke but he couldn't hear what he was saying. Not that Cain cared one whit. He was on a mission and nothing and no one was going to get in his way. His woman was back at the cabin all battered and bruised and there was no way he was letting that fucking asshole get away with what he'd done to the love of his life.

Cain growled when those pictures gracing the wall of Arty's cabin flashed in his mind again. He didn't think he'd ever get over seeing her beautiful naked body pinned up on that wall. How many times had that demented fucker jacked off while looking at his girl?

Another snarl tore from his mouth and he took great gulping breaths, trying to calm the rage permeating his body and soul. He was so angry he was literally seeing through a red haze.

When he caught sight of a group of hands heading back from the far north end of the property he scanned the group looking for the little fucker. Cain finally spotted him toward the back of the group, and with a slight nudge of his knee he sent his horse into the middle of the hands.

Arty saw Cain coming and his face paled but not once did the asshole's expression change. When he was a few feet away from him, Cain kicked one foot free of the stirrups and launched himself off his mount toward Arty. He grabbed hold of the bastard's shirt and sent them both tumbling to the ground. Cain landed on top of him and heard him gasp and groan as the air was knocked from his lungs.

Cain fisted the prick's shirt, drew his fist back, and let fly. He pounded on him over and over again, and if it hadn't been for Danny, Luke, and Damon pulling him off of him, he probably would have ended up killing the bastard. He shook and quivered, pushing against the hold Danny and Damon had on him, until finally his breathing slowed and the red haze left his eyes. When he came back to himself he grunted with satisfaction to see that he had busted Arty's nose and his face was bruised and swollen. Luke quickly restrained Arty in cuffs and between him and Damon got him back on his horse belly and face down.

"Are you all right now?" Luke asked.

Cain nodded and turned back to his horse.

"You're lucky you didn't kill him. I would have hated to arrest your ass."

Cain shrugged but sighed. He was glad he hadn't killed Arty either because he needed to spend the rest of his days loving Cash.

Danny clapped him on the shoulder. "I think it was a good thing you got to him first because I don't know if I would have been able to stop."

"I wouldn't have either if it hadn't been for you and those two damn sheriffs."

Danny slapped him on the back. "Let's go be with our woman. She needs us, Cain."

Cain nodded, mounted up and headed back to Cash.

* * * *

Bruce removed the leather from her wrists while Cain and Danny worked on getting her ankles free. After carefully lowering her arms he pulled his shirt off over his head and with his brothers' help pulled it over her head and pushed her arms through the sleeves. There was a long cut on the side of her head and she was covered in blood from there down, over the side of her face and down her neck, but she was alive. He checked her over for other injuries and was relieved when he couldn't find any, but he was getting real worried because she hadn't woken up.

"Cash, can you hear me? Come on, sweet cheeks, let me see those beautiful eyes."

Cash sighed and frowned and then mumbled but Bruce couldn't hear what she said.

"Cashmere, look at me," Cain demanded and Bruce gripped her hand when her eyelids fluttered open.

"You found me. Arty…"

"Shh, sugar." Danny sat near her feet and stroked her leg. "You're safe now, he can't hurt you anymore."

"I love you," Cash whispered. "I never thought I'd see you again. I love you all so much."

Bruce carefully gathered her into his arms when she began to cry and held her tight. The paramedics came and assessed Cash. She didn't want to go to the clinic but she needed stitches and probably had a concussion from the hit to the head. He didn't give in to her nonsense or argue with her, he just picked her up and carried her into the ambulance.

As the doors closed he saw Luke and Damon carting a handcuffed Arty away and hoped the bastard would rot in jail. He held her hand the entire way to the clinic and even while the doc cleaned and stitched her up. Cain and Danny came bursting through the doors and immediately came over to Cash's side.

"Okay, all done young lady. I'm letting you go home since I know these three will take care of you." The doctor looked at Bruce and he nodded in affirmation. "Wake her every couple of hours for the first twenty four. If the pain gets worse or she's sick call me. Day or night. Or if you're worried about anything. If the headache hasn't let up by the day after tomorrow bring her back or give me a call, and don't get those stitches wet. I'll take them out in seven days. Any questions?"

"No, thanks doc." Bruce shook his hand and then picked Cash up. She rested her head against his shoulder and closed her eyes.

When they got back to the ranch Luke was waiting on the porch. He followed them inside and headed for the kitchen. Cain rushed to the bedroom and brought a pillow out from Cash's bed while Danny went and got a spare quilt. Bruce helped her settle on the sofa and within minutes she was fast asleep. Luke brought out coffee for everyone except Cash and sat in one of the armchairs.

"I finally got the report back on the prints, although we don't need them now. We were damn lucky to get to Cash when we did. It turns out that Arty is a psychopath and has been in and out of mental institutions his whole life. He killed his mother when he was just in his late teens and was brought in for questioning when other women disappeared while he was in the vicinity, but there was never any evidence found to arrest him."

"Jesus," Bruce said and placed his hand on Cash's leg. He was sitting on the couch near her feet. Cain was in the corner near her head and Danny was on the floor looking uncomfortable in his twisted position with his hand on her hip.

"I don't think this case will end up at trial. Arty will be assessed and hopefully shut away in a high-security mental institution for the rest of his life."

"Thank God," Cain growled.

"I'm going to need a statement from Cash when she's up to it. Call me when you think she's ready." Luke drained the last of his coffee and then headed out. Bruce didn't bother to get up because he didn't want to leave Cash's side.

At least now they wouldn't have to worry about Arty making bail in a few years and coming back for their woman. The tension which had been invading his muscles drained away as he stared at her beautiful face. Cash had finally admitted her love for them and now he and his brothers could look forward to spending the rest of their lives living with and loving their woman. All they had to do was pack up their ranch and move to Slick Rock. He couldn't wait.

"Call our foreman and get the men to start organizing the ranch." Bruce nodded to Danny. "Make sure you tell him that anyone who wants to move will be covered in our expenses and anyone who doesn't will get a generous payout. We'll start searching the net for some land and go from there."

Chapter Twelve

It had been two weeks since Arty had clocked her on the head and tied her up and she had spent each and every night of the last two weeks sleeping between her three men. She'd had the stitches out a week ago and still none of her men had tried to make love with her. Cash was getting a little frustrated but figured that her men were scared to touch her in case they hurt her, but she was totally healed and had had the all clear from the doctor.

One of them had stayed with her since that frightful day and kept an eye on her and the ranch, but the other two not babysitting her disappeared for hours on end. They were up to something but she had no idea what. When she'd asked the only answer she got was that they had been busy making sure things were running smoothly out on the land, but she knew they were lying. Neither Bruce, Cain, nor Danny looked her in the eye when they replied, and Cash was becoming a little paranoid. Thoughts of them having another woman lodged in her head, and no matter how hard she tried to dispel that notion, it wouldn't budge.

Clay, Johnny, and Tara were due back sometime today from their vacation and Cash was beginning to feel sick at the thought of her men going back to their own home over four hours away. Were they going to just up and leave without asking her to go with them? Her heart was aching and even though she wanted to come right out and ask them if they still wanted her, she was afraid of the answer, so she kept her mouth shut.

Cash concentrated on running the brush through the horse's coat, the repetitive action soothing as her mind ran round in circles of turmoil. Truck doors slammed and then she heard her boss's voices. The roiling in her gut got worse. Her heart was beating so hard she thought it just might jump out of her chest. All three of her men were here today and she figured that was because of their cousins' return. She wanted to go out and see what everyone was doing but she didn't want to interrupt the family reunion. After finishing up with the horse she was grooming she gathered up the bucket of supplies and moved toward the next stall. It had been half an hour since the Morten's had arrived home and she wondered what was going on. Usually the first thing Clay did when he came home from somewhere was check the barn, but this time he didn't even pop his head in.

Cash hoped that Bruce, Cain and Danny hadn't told them about what Arty had tried to do to her but she knew that was wishful thinking. Of course the men would have to tell the owners why one of their ranch hands was no longer around. Would they blame her for losing one of their workers?

Stop it, Cash. They won't blame you. Clay and Johnny would be really angry about what happened. They protect the women of this town. Even she knew that all the men in Slick Rock banded together to keep the women and children safe. *God, I'm going out of my mind.*

She looked up when she heard someone enter the barn and saw Clay striding toward her. *Is he angry? He looks angry. Is he going to fire me? What am I going to do if he does?* It looked like her men had been organizing to leave as soon as their cousins got home—she'd seen the packed bags and the boxes they stowed into their truck—and she was worried they were going to leave her behind.

"Cash, are you okay, honey?" Clay asked as he grabbed the bucket from her hand and dropped it on the ground. He gripped her shoulders and pulled her into a hug.

"I'm fine," she mumbled into his chest.

"I'm so sorry, Cash. We had no idea that Arty was insane. We never would have hired him otherwise."

"Not your fault."

"It sure as shit is," Clay grumbled. "We always do background checks but we didn't with him, just took his word for it and hired him since we were in desperate need for another hand. I figured that I would look into him if he didn't work hard or didn't get along with the other hands. He sure fooled us all."

Clay released her and took a step back. "You look okay. Are you sure you should be working yet?"

"The doc gave me the all clear."

"Well, just let me know if you get tired and I'll get someone to take over your chores."

"Thanks, but I'm fine."

Clay nodded, looked toward the entrance and then back to her. "I don't want you working today. In fact I want you to take some time off."

Cash opened her mouth but closed it again when he held up his hand. "Don't argue with me Cash, I'm the boss and what I say goes."

Cash lowered her head so he wouldn't see the tears in her eyes. It looked like she was right. He didn't want her working for him anymore. He was probably worried about her being the only female hand and the trouble she'd caused because of her gender. She gave a nod of her head, picked the bucket up and took it to the tack room. After depositing it on the shelf she came back out, but Clay was nowhere to be seen. She shuffled her feet on the dirt floor dejectedly and made her way toward the exit. Quickly wiping the tears from her face she glanced around and noted that no one was close enough to see her crying, thankfully, and headed toward her cabin.

She opened her front door and her shoulders slumped when she saw the suitcase near the door. She didn't have to open it to know that all her things were in there. It looked like she was being fired after all. Giving one last look around the home she had for the last twelve months, she picked up her case, quietly closed the door and walked toward her car.

She was only halfway to where her car was parked when a large hand covered hers and took the case handle from her. She gave a sideways look and saw Bruce walking beside her. Her heart broke in two and emotion clogged her throat, but she wasn't about to let him know how hurt she was. Without saying a word or even looking at her Bruce opened the back door to her car and put her case in.

Cash removed her car keys from her pocket and choked back a sob. It was kind of Bruce to carry her bag for her but she longed to see Cain and Danny before she left. It seemed that wasn't to be. She obviously wasn't as important to them as they were to her.

She opened the front door and went to get in but Bruce clasped her wrist and took the keys from her hand. He guided her around to the passenger seat and after buckling her in, he skirted the back of her car and then got in the driver's seat.

Cash stared at him as he released the lever and pushed the seat back as far as it would go. He never once looked at her or spoke and then he started her car and backed it out of the carport.

When he got to the end of the drive he turned left, away from Slick Rock. She couldn't stand the silence one more minute and even though she was scared of the answer she had to ask the question.

"What's going on?" She cursed under her breath because even she could hear the pain in the hoarseness of her own voice.

"You'll know in a minute," Bruce replied cryptically.

Cash turned back to stare out the windscreen and then gasped fifteen minutes later when Bruce slowed her car and turned in another long gravel driveway. She glimpsed a new sign hanging on the gate but wasn't sure she had seen right. Turning her head, trying to see the sign again, she gave up a moment later because trees now obscured the sign. She gave a shake of her head and knew she couldn't have seen what she thought. It was probably wishful thinking on her behalf.

Bruce slowed her car and pulled it up close to the house. "Are we visiting someone?"

"You could say that."

Cash reached for the door handle but Bruce stopped her. "Wait for me to get your door, Cash."

She slumped back against her seat and watched as he got out and walked around the car. When he opened the door and held out his hand, she looked up into his gleaming eyes and gulped. *God, I'm going to miss him and his brothers so much. How will I survive never seeing them again?*

Cash gulped again and then placed her hand in his. Bruce helped her from the car and led her up the porch steps toward the front door.

"So what do you think of the place?"

"It's nice," Cash answered honestly. "I've been here before."

"Yeah, I know. We've heard all about how you used your down time to come and help Mr. Bowen with his chores. Did you know that he wanted to sell up so he could move closer to his kids?"

"Yes, he talked about his daughters all the time, but he loves this ranch, even if it was getting too much for him to keep up."

"So why are we here? Did he invite us over?"

"No."

Cash dug her heels in but Bruce was so big and strong she didn't stand a chance of stopping him. Just as they reached the front door it swung open and she was surprised to see Danny and Cain inside the house.

"Did you tell…" Cain began but Bruce interrupted him.

"Nope."

"So she thinks…" Danny started.

"Yep."

Bruce pulled her across the threshold, ignoring the fact that she was tugging hard, trying to get free.

Cash looked back at the door when it was closed behind her and then turned to face Bruce, Cain and Danny again. "What the hell is wrong with you? We can't just barge in here uninvited. Mr. Bowen is going to have a fit."

"He's not here, baby," Cain said.

"Where is he? We shouldn't be here." Cash spun around, intending to leave, but Bruce snagged an arm around her waist and lifted her feet from the floor with ease. She kicked out with her feet, trying to get him to release her but she should have known it was impossible against such a big brute. His nickname was Brutus after all.

Bruce carried her over to the sofa and plunked her down on a cushion. All three men crouched down in front of her. Danny and Cain each took one of her hands in one of theirs.

"You aren't going to be working for our cousins' anymore, sugar," Danny said. Cash felt moisture prick the back of her eyes and she could have cheerfully hit him when she saw the gleam in his.

"He's firing me?" Cash asked, cursing the hitch in her voice.

"No," Danny replied, and at the same time Cain said, "Yes," and Bruce said, "In a way."

"It's because of what happened with Arty, isn't it?" Cash couldn't stop the sob that erupted from her mouth and tears leaked from her eyes and down her cheeks.

"No, sweet cheeks, you won't be working there anymore because of us," Bruce answered.

"What? You got me fired? Why the hell would you do something like that?"

"Because we love you, Cashmere Woodall and we want to spend the rest of our lives with you."

Cash's heart fluttered and began to fill with hope. The dejectedness she had been feeling dissipated and in its place joy reined.

"You do?" she whispered.

"Yeah, sweet cheeks, we do." Bruce reached into his shirt pocket and palmed something in his hand. He fiddled with whatever it was and then held his hand out flat.

Cash gasped, and if she'd had a hand free she would have placed it over her racing heart.

"Sugar." Danny's voice drew her gaze and tears filled her eyes when she saw the emotion in his eyes. "I love you more than I can say. Will you marry me?"

"Baby." Cain's gravelly voice sent shivers up her spine. "I love you and don't want to spend another minute away from you. Will you marry me?"

"Sweet cheeks." Bruce's deep cadence caused goose bumps to rise up on her skin. "You are the air I breathe. Will you marry me?"

The tears she been trying to hold at bay overflowed and tracked down her face. Love and joy filled her heart and she nearly yelled her answer. "Yes! God, I love you all so much. I didn't think you wanted me anymore."

Cash glanced down to her hand when Bruce took it from Cain and then slid the ring onto her finger. He scooped her up into his arms, carrying her from the living room toward the bedrooms.

"What are you doing?" she asked as she clung to his neck.

Bruce kissed her temple but kept right on going. "You're home now, sweet cheeks, and you're never leaving our sides again."

"Home?"

"Yeah," Cain answered and moved in behind her when Bruce lowered her feet to the floor.

"This is our home now, sugar, and we can't wait to start the rest of our lives."

"Ours?"

Bruce reached out and cupped her face between her hands. "Ours, Cash. Mr. Bowen sold us his ranch and since we knew that our relationship wouldn't be accepted back home we relocated our operation here. Welcome home to the Triple M Ranch, sweet cheeks."

Cash sobbed with happiness but the sound was muffled when Bruce covered her mouth with his. She stood up on tiptoes and wrapped her arms around his neck and gave herself over to her men.

His tongue glided over her lips and she opened to him instantly. Hands tugged at her clothes and moved her arms but she kept right on kissing Bruce. She shivered with desire as three pairs of hands caressed her now-naked body. When Bruce finally lifted his head they were both panting for breath. Cash glanced toward the massive bed and then climbed up onto it on her back and spread her arms and legs wide. Her men practically tore their clothes from their bodies in their rush to get to her.

Cain was the first one to get naked, and instead of getting on the bed he dove onto it and landed right between her legs. He gave her a sexy smile and wink and then lowered his head. She cried out when his tongue swiped through her folds and then lapped at her clit. The mattress dipped on either side of her, and as she reached down to thread her fingers into Cain's hair, Danny cupped her face and stared into her eyes.

"I love you." She didn't get the chance to reply because he kissed her. Danny made love to her mouth like he was starving and if he felt anything like she did, then he was. It had been two long weeks since they had made love for the first time and she couldn't wait to have all of her men inside her. She moaned when Bruce began suckling on her breast and arched her body up into her men's touch.

Cain growled against her pussy and then pushed a finger inside her. Cash's gasp of pleasure was muffled by Danny's mouth. When Cain began to pump his finger in and out of her rapidly she knew it wouldn't take long for her to fly. Already her insides were coiling with the pleasurable friction and when Cain sucked on her clit she screamed as the orgasm washed over her. He didn't let up his sucking or pumping finger until the last shudder faded.

"I love it when you come, baby. I could eat that delectable cream for hours on end." Cain sat up between her thighs and wiped his mouth and chin.

"Oh God."

"Turn over, sweet cheeks," Bruce demanded after lifting his head from her breast, and then all three of her men helped her onto her stomach.

Cain clasped her hips and shoved a pillow under them. "We need to prepare you, baby. We don't want to hurt you when we take you together."

"Yes! I need you all so much."

"And you'll have us soon, sugar." Danny gripped her hair and turned her face toward him. "Stay nice and relaxed so Cain can get your ass ready. Keep your eyes on me, Cash."

She nodded and took a deep breath when she heard a pop and knew that Cain had opened a bottle of lube.

"Try not to tense up, baby."

Cash shivered when her ass cheeks were spread wide and cold wet fingers began to massage her rosette.

"Would you look at that ass," Bruce rumbled. "Such a nice ripe-looking peach."

She whimpered when the tip of Cain's finger pushed into her asshole. The pinch and burn was overridden as nerve endings lit up and morphed to pleasure. He took his time with her, adding more lube as he stretched her out. By the time he had three fingers in her bottom Cash was gasping for breath and on the verge of another climax.

"Please."

"Please what, sweet cheeks?" Bruce panted.

"Please make love to me," she begged.

"With pleasure." Cain growled from behind her and then withdrew his finger from her ass. She heard foil packs ripping and then she was pulled up to her hands and knees. When the tip of Cain's condom-covered cock began to press into her dark entrance, Cash concentrated on her breathing and trying to stay relaxed. The large blunt head of his penis pushed through the first tight ring and then he held still.

"All right, baby?"

"Yes. I need more."

"We'll give you more, sugar." Danny kissed her lips. "Let Cain get into that sexy butt and then you'll have all the cock you want."

Bruce reached under her and squeezed a nipple, sending zings down to her pussy. She clenched and cream dripped from her cunt.

"Jesus," Cain gasped. "Wait until I'm all the way inside her before you do that again. She's squeezing me so fucking hard. Your ass is heaven, baby."

Cash groaned. Her body was shaking with need and the fire inside her was building too fast. Her ass felt like it was stretched wide and even though it burned it felt so good she didn't want Cain to stop.

"I'm in, Cash." Cain panted against her ear. She held onto his forearms when he pulled her back up against his front and then he slowly lowered down to the bed on his back and she was lying on top of him with her legs draped over his. Cain spread his legs wide, opening her up, exposing her pussy.

Danny crawled up between her legs, his hands on the mattress on either side of her shoulders. He stared down at her with such love in his eyes and she felt so connected to him, to all of them and he wasn't even inside her yet.

"Are you ready for me, sugar?"

"Yes. Now. I want all of you. Hurry."

Danny leaned down and kissed her long and deep. As he made love to her mouth she felt his cock against her pussy, and then he was pushing inside her. Cash whimpered with pleasure as he slowly worked his dick into her vagina. Her internal walls rippled and she covered him in her juices.

"So good, sugar. I've never felt anything this fucking good." Danny pushed up from over her and sat up between her splayed legs.

"Me neither." She gasped when Danny withdrew until just the tip of his cock was inside her, and then shoved forward. As he slid into her, Cain pulled nearly all the way out of her ass. The two men started off slow, letting her get used to having two cocks fucking her ass and pussy, but she still wasn't complete.

Turning her head her gaze latched onto Bruce's big hard cock. He was lying on his side with a pillow under his hip and sort of curved around the top of her and Danny. It put him in the optimum position for what she wanted to do. Reaching out, she wrapped her hand around his shaft but growled with frustration when his cock didn't reach her mouth.

Bruce got up onto his knees and bent over her. She smiled up into his eyes and kept them connected with his as she licked around the broad bulbous head. "Oh fuck yeah, sweet cheeks. That feels so damn good. Suck my cock, Cash."

Cash opened her mouth wide and sucked him down. She took him in as far as she could, hollowed out her cheeks as she pulled back up over his length, and then laved the underside with her tongue. She froze when Cain surged back into her ass.

"Let me, Cash." Bruce gripped the base of his cock and waited. Cash opened her mouth into an *O* and sighed as he began to fuck her mouth. She groaned and sighed with bliss as her three men made love to her.

Cain and Danny set up a rhythm of advance and retreat, counter thrusting in and out of her body and Bruce set one up all of his own. With each surge and rock of their hips the tension inside her grew. Saliva dribbled onto her chin as she sucked Bruce's cock and even though he was pumping his hips quickly, he never once went too far and made her choke.

Molten liquid spread through her body, centering in her womb, making it feel heavy as cream wept from her pussy. The coils inside her grew tauter and tauter until she was on the edge of something so big it rocked her to her core.

And then she was there, hanging on the edge of the precipice by her fingertips. Cash let go, knowing her men would catch her and screamed as rapture engulfed her. Her body shook and shuddered, quaked and quavered as she climaxed. Her heart and soul soared into the stratosphere, disbanding every cell in her body and then slamming them back together again, making her feel complete for the first time in her life.

"I'm gonna come, Cash." Bruce gasped. "Swallow me."

Bruce roared as his cock jerked in her mouth, spewing his essence over her tongue and down her throat. Cash gulped down his seed, relishing the salty, spicy taste of his cum and not wanting to lose a drop. He withdrew from her mouth and collapsed on the bed beside her, panting heavily.

"Oh Jesus. So fucking good," Danny rasped. "Here I come, sugar."

Danny gripped her hips firmly, forged his way into her pussy one more time and jerked above her as he reached his peak.

"My turn," Cain growled. He slammed into her twice more and shouted. "Ah!"

Cain's cock thickened inside her and then he spewed his cum into the end of the condom. The heat of his seed and the pulsing of his cock sent her into another climax. Cash had no breath left and opened her mouth on a soundless cry.

"Fucking heaven, baby," Cain panted, gripped her chin, turned her head and kissed her on the mouth and then caused them to both groan when he gently pulled from her body and relaxed beneath her.

Danny rolled them both to their sides and withdrew from her pussy. Bruce shoved his brothers out of the way and lifted her into his arms. "How about a bath in your new bathroom, sweet cheeks?"

"That sounds nice."

"So when do you want to get married, Cash?" Cain asked and she looked over her shoulder to see him and Danny following them into the bathroom.

"Whenever you want."

"How 'bout tomorrow, sugar?"

"Tomorrow? Really?"

"Yeah." Bruce grinned and sat down on the rim of the large beautiful spa bath, placing her on his lap. He reached over and turned the faucets on. "It's all been arranged."

"It has?"

"Yes, Cash, it has," Cain said in a deep growly voice, looking a little uncertain of her reaction. In fact, when she looked at each of her men, it warmed her heart to know that none of them were confident of her answer.

She gave them a smile and let the love for her men shine from her eyes.

"Tomorrow." Cash nodded her head. "I can't wait."

Her men cheered, hugged her, and kissed her.

Cash had so much to look forward to, a new home to explore with the loves of her life by her side and long happy years to show them how much she loved them in return.

She couldn't have asked for anything more.

THE END

WWW.BECCAVAN-EROTICROMANCE.COM

ABOUT THE AUTHOR

My name is Becca Van. I live in Australia with my wonderful hubby of many years, as well as my two children.

I read my first romance, which I found in the school library, at the age of thirteen and haven't stopped reading them since. It is so wonderful to know that love is still alive and strong when there seems to be so much conflict in the world.

I dreamed of writing my own book one day but, unfortunately, didn't follow my dream for many years. But once I started I knew writing was what I wanted to continue doing.

I love to escape from the world and curl up with a good romance, to see how the characters unfold and conflict is dealt with. I have read many books and love all facets of the romance genre, from historical to erotic romance. I am a sucker for a happy ending.

For all titles by Becca Van, please visit
www.bookstrand.com/becca-van

Siren Publishing, Inc.
www.SirenPublishing.com

CPSIA information can be obtained at www.ICGtesting.com
Printed in the USA
LVOW10s2110110315

430147LV00022B/538/P